ONLY
BIG BUMBUM
MATTERS
TOMORROW

ALSO BY DAMILARE KUKU

Nearly All the Men in Lagos Are Mad: Stories

ONLY BIG BUMBUM MATTERS TOMORROW

A NOVEL

DAMILARE KUKU

HarperVia

An Imprint of HarperCollins*Publishers*

HarperCollins books may be purchased for educational, business, or sales
promotional use. For information, please email the Special Markets Department at SPsales@harpercollins.com.

FIRST EDITION

Designed by Janet Evans-Scanlon

Library of Congress Cataloging-in-Publication Data
Names: Kuku, Damilare, author.
Title: Only big bumbum matters tomorrow : a novel / Damilare Kuku.
Description: First edition. | New York, NY : HarperVia, an imprint of
    HarperCollins Publisher, 2024. |
Identifiers: LCCN 2023056571 (print) | LCCN 2023056572 (ebook) | ISBN
    9780063354494 (hardcover) | ISBN 9780063354517 (ebook)
Subjects: LCGFT: Novels.
Classification: LCC PR9387.9.K85 O55 2024 (print) | LCC PR9387.9.K85
    (ebook) | DDC 823.92—dc23/eng/20231208
LC record available at https://lccn.loc.gov/2023056571
LC ebook record available at https://lccn.loc.gov/2023056572

24 25 26 27 28 LBC 5 4 3 2 1

For the ones like me who stare at a mirror all day
hoping to fix it all with their eyes . . .
I have broken my mirror, please break yours.

Also for Olúrẹ̀mí Àbákẹ́
Òrìsà bí ìyá, kò sí láyẹ́.

CONTENTS

Prologue 1

TODAY, THIS SMALL YANSH MUST GO! 3

Témì Is a Blackboard 5

Ládùn, the Outsider 30

Hassana's Womb 42

Jummai, the Big Mouth 48

Big Mummy Is Not Angry 52

Barrister's Belly 59

**YESTERDAY, AND THE BODIES THAT
WALKED THROUGH IT** 63

Témì Is Also a Mopstick! 65

Ládùn's Body 88

Jummai Is Plenty 110

Hassana's Face 117

OMOLÁDÙN AYÉ AND HER FIVE YEARS 135

Hassana's Children 137

Ládùn and Lagos 154

Témì's Silence 172

Ládùn and Edache 180

Témì 194

Jummai's Truth 212

CONTENTS

TOMORROW, WE SAVE TÉMÌ 227

Dr. Anyadike's Opinion Matters 229

Prophet, Please Pray It Away! 234

Big Sister Ládùn 236

Témì 240

Author's Note 253

Acknowledgements 255

A Note on the Cover 259

ONLY
BIG BUMBUM
MATTERS
TOMORROW

PROLOGUE

"I plan to renovate my bumbum in Lagos, live there for some time, and hopefully meet the love of my life!"

You had hoped your clever use of the word "renovate" would douse the tension in the room, elicit a smile from those assembled, perhaps even fits of laughter. Instead, you saw your mother digging her big toe into the old living room rug, the red nail paint chipping as she dug deeper.

Silence.

"Ehn? Témì, ṣé o ti bẹ̀rẹ̀ sí í mu igbó ni? Have you started smoking weed? Why would you do that?" Aunty Jummai barked at you while retying her wrapper. The smoke from the jollof rice cooking in the kitchen caused her eyes to water.

A ringtone was hastily silenced; someone muffled a cough. The lawyer who had been getting ready to take his leave sank deeper into the chair your father had loved.

"No, Aunty. Smoking kills. Would I fix my buttocks if I wanted to die young? I am doing it because I want to—it's my body," you answered as truthfully as you could.

Now you were stuck in the house, with no chance of fleeing

the slow fire that was burning within your family. You were unlikely to make the consultation scheduled for ten days' time.

Nigerian families can be an obstacle in a girl's journey to a figure eight.

part one

TODAY, THIS SMALL YANSH MUST GO!

TÉMÌ IS A BLACKBOARD

Your bumbum has always been flat.

You stared, as usual, hoping that some fat had miraculously found its way into it. In your midi midnight-blue lace dress, you looked at your slender frame in the full-length mirror that stood next to your bed. You lifted one hand to clutch both breasts and touched the small of your back with the other. If only your ass was bigger, your tiny waist would have been a magnet for compliments. You dropped both hands and sighed. This was your morning ritual. For yourself. For your sanity. For your sense of somebodiness.

You looked at the window opposite your bed and made a mental note to dust it and wash the curtains that hung loosely by its sides.

You thought about what you planned to do. You thought about your family.

You sighed again.

How do you inform your family members that you intend to surgically enlarge your buttocks without receiving a barrage of curses? How do you slip it into a conversation with Màámi that you intend to relocate to Lagos to meet the man who will love you senseless? How do you tell your older sister, who, until a week ago, you hadn't seen in five years, that you are hoping to stay in her Lagos apartment while you recover from surgery, maybe even stay a few more months? How?

These questions had been nagging at you since you decided to take the big step to redeem your backside. Time was not your friend; you needed to make the announcement quickly if you were to cash in on the new Easter discount you had seen on Instagram yesterday. The advertisement was clear and straight to the point:

> **Laydiz, this is for you!**
> **This offer lasts till the end of the month.**
> **So if you really want to enter Easter with a snatched body,**
> **now is the time to go for it.**
> **For my slim laydiz, BBL is possible!**
> **For my thick laydiz, BBL is possible!**
> **Fillers, BBL, nonsurgical butt lift . . . this clinic has got you!**
> **Don't go to where they will not shape your yansh well o.**

You loved the hearty salesmanship of the clinic's brand ambassador, even with her confusing accent and nude-glossed lips that parted to reveal the whitest teeth you had ever seen. She probably had veneers. You beamed at your phone, using the screen as a mirror to assess your own teeth. They were not shockingly white, but white enough, thanks to your mother who brushed your teeth with pákò when you were a child, before using a toothbrush with toothpaste.

Good personal hygiene was a virtue that was nonnegotiable for Màámi. Her favourite quote had always been "A woman's parts should be clean and her breath fresh." She would scold you mildly whenever she noticed a speck of imperfection. "Témì, I can still see the soap on your body. Go back and give yourself another rinse. Ládùn, go and supervise your sister." Most times, the supervision ended in a splashing contest between you and your sister, until one of your parents broke it off. It was of utmost importance that you scrubbed thoroughly with kànrìnkàn and rinsed with water.

The bumbum-enlargement advert continued playing. The presenter, Sylvia Osuji, an alumna of your university, was now an influencer. She spoke glowingly of the ongoing Easter offer, sharing with great enthusiasm how she saved up for her surgery, how her decision to go under the knife was the best she had ever made, and how her ass now attracted the high-and-mighty. "Use what you have to get what you want," she crowed. Sylvia was an acquaintance from your university days, so you had no qualms about going to a clinic she had recommended. While Sylvia was a year ahead of you, she had never been high on the social ladder and mostly stayed in the shadows. However, since graduating, she had been winning in every circle, all because of that new ass.

The first time you saw her video, you sent it straight to your friend. "Bọbọọlá, you know we are about to graduate. I think it's time we upgraded ourselves like Sylvia."

"Témì, I agree. I swear, I was just thinking about it. Dis my yansh no gree grow."

Her eagerness made you uneasy. "Don't you want to think about it?"

"Nope. I'm down," she responded.

"It's just our parents I'm worried about."

"Must they know? And as long as they are not paying, mine couldn't care less."

"Who will pay for yours?" you asked.

"You know that man that has been sending me messages on Twitter? I checked his profile. He has money. If he wants to date me, he will pay. Yours?"

"I am not sure."

"Témì, we have been confined to Ifè all our lives. If we must move, let us start making decisions on our own."

"Perhaps I could tell my daddy after we graduate. He's actually cool about these things. It is Màámi that could pose a challenge. For now, we should do proper research on the procedure. Maybe we should go with the clinic that Sylvia used."

"That clinic is expensive, Témì. Do you have three million naira? I don't think I can get more than one million from all my boyfriends combined. I hope this Twitter guy comes through. Let me start replying to his DMs now."

"Bòbóólá, please, let's just wait. We will find a way."

"Okay, we'll wait."

The verbal agreement clearly meant nothing to Bòbóólá because she resumed the final semester with an enlarged ass. "I ate a lot of protein during the Covid-19 break, and I wore a waist trainer every day," Bòbóólá told each girl who asked.

"Please share your diet with me. I need my backside to start confusing my boyfriend," your school friends pleaded.

You saw them perching around her like she was a messiah, hanging on her every word. You wondered if it was the protein that shaped her ass like a perfect apple and cinched her waist.

Protein must be a miracle worker that only favoured Bọbọọlá. Bọbọọlá's betrayal showed that you never really knew people, even if you had been best friends for over ten years.

This made her recent visits all the more unexpected. You didn't invite her or anyone else when your daddy died. At least *she* could claim that she used to be your friend; the others were mere neighbourhood acquaintances. One example was Sọlá, whose family had moved next door when his father became a professor, and to whom all you ever said was the occasional half-hearted greeting.

The day you went with your parents to welcome them, Sọlá's mother said, "You people should be friends! Témì looks like a good girl. Just see how nice you look together." You knew this tired line well. The African parent's go-to attempt at subtle matchmaking.

You and Sọlá exchanged numbers, but you both knew it was unlikely either would get in touch. He was the sort of guy who moved with the club guys on campus, the ones whose parents sent them to federal universities to humble them but still gave them a comfortable-enough life to make up for not going abroad for university. Until recently, you had no reason to spend time together.

Thankfully, you were too busy with errands to deal with the unwelcome mourners. Besides, Ládùn's presence kept everyone's mouth busy. Hushed whispers travelled through the air every day whenever she showed her face at the house. The prodigal child had returned!

"Témì, is that Ládùn? Damn! She is so fine!" Sọlá had spoken into your left ear while everyone was singing the final hymn in church. The simp had forgotten that he had been shoving his tongue down your throat just earlier that day. He had also forgotten funerals were not for flirting, or maybe he had never cared about decency.

"I am in love. Maybe *she* is the sister for me. As you no gree for me."

"Ṣọlá, please sing the hymn," you hissed as the organ struck a chord that had the choir singing louder, masking your reprimand. Your eyes travelled to Ládùn, who stood beside Màámi at the altar, where they were receiving prayers on behalf of the family.

Ládùn and Màámi could easily be mistaken for twins. They wore matching Ankara styles—body-fitting gowns with aṣọ òkè adorning the fronts of their dresses. Although grief had given her a hunched back, Màámi's beauty was the kind you had to take in slowly and repeatedly, to be sure she was not a drawing. Graceful as a swan, Ládùn was not fair-skinned like your mother, but she also wasn't the colour of the night, as you were. She had your mother's face, but all her mannerisms were your father's. Trust Ládùn to steal the shine even after many years of being away. *Your* face was a perfect mix of your parents', and thankfully, you took each of their best features: your father's full lips and sleepy, catlike eyes and your mother's pointed nose and brownish-pink lips, but it didn't make people stare at you the way they stared at Màámi and Ládùn. If you didn't love your sister so much, you would have hated her.

Suddenly, your phone buzzed. Sylvia the Influencer had just posted another picture, showing her before-and-after bodies, reminding you of your present dilemma—how to inform your family of the decision to embellish your bumbum. You closed

Instagram and opened the banking app to check your account balance. After saving for nearly two years, you had two million naira, thanks to a lucrative side hustle and Daddy's generosity.

At your graduation the year before, your father had asked what you wanted, eager to reward you for your First-Class Honours, but you couldn't bring yourself to say it. Since Ládùn had left, they treated you like they were afraid you would leave too. Why else would anyone throw such a lavish graduation party and hire a famous musician like Yínká Ayéfẹ́lẹ́, who only performed at big society events? The music from your party nearly drowned out other parents' celebrations. Ayéfẹ́lẹ́ serenaded the guests with the talking drum, singing your praises. Màámi sang along with him, giddy with excitement, like a schoolgirl.

Mo gbọ́ wípé many people
Wón ní wí pé many people saaaayyyy...
still Ayéfẹ́lẹ́ o le dìde

"Màámi, must Yínká Ayéfẹ́lẹ́ sing so loudly?"

"Ehn ehn, would you rather he whispered? After we paid him so much?" She twirled under the rented canopy.

An hour into Ayéfẹ́lẹ́'s performance, other graduands came to the canopy that your family had installed in the middle of the field. They celebrated with you, resigned to the fact that no one could outshine your mother. As you welcomed and served strangers, you remembered that Ládùn's graduation was celebrated with a dinner that your father missed because he was attending a ceremony with the vice chancellor in Àkúré. Ládùn left for Lagos that night. Yet here they were—giving out gift bags as souvenirs and smiling sheepishly.

"Témì, what do you want, dear?" your father repeated in his airy voice. He was serious.

A new bumbum will be great, sir, you wanted to say. But you replied, "I am fine, Daddy."

"Témì, come and dance with your mother," Màámi called.

"Màámi—" A lump formed in your throat as you hesitated.

"Just come, my brilliant baby." Màámi dragged you to the dance floor.

Aunty Jummai was serving food and receiving congratulatory messages as if she was the mother of the child graduating. Sometimes you felt she acted outlandishly, hoping to get a reaction from your mother. Your mother ignored her, as usual.

You spent the rest of the day avoiding unsolicited prayers from well-wishers. "After this graduation, your husband will locate you!" "Children will locate you!" "You will find a good job!" "You will get a visa to travel and leave this country!" Their prayers were spoken in between mouthfuls of succulent meat, while you tried your best to avoid their spittle hitting your forehead.

"Amen!"

The next time that you felt confident enough to tell your parents about your desired gift was a quiet evening after the usual family devotion. As your father relaxed into his chair, fanning himself with the newspaper he had read earlier in the day, Màámi and Aunty Jummai cracked melon seeds over a wooden tray at the dining table. You were seated close to your father in the living room.

"Daddy, Màámi, I want—"

Aunty Jummai cut in. "My professor, I have been meaning to discuss the recent strike with you—"

"Jummai, Témì was about to say something," Màámi interjected.

Aunty Jummai's eyes flared. "And I should keep quiet for her?"

Màámi got up as if scorched by Aunty Jummai's eyes and walked toward you.

"No, Màámi, it is not important." You were already tired.

"Are you sure?" Your daddy enquired with a smile. "Is it money?"

"No, I'll be in my room." Your exhaustion had peaked.

"Okay, dear. Let's give your dad and your aunty room to continue their conversation."

As you and your mother walked into the corridor, Aunty Jummai resumed. "They are also helping the government to waste their time. It is bad enough that the ASUU is always going on strike. Now the students want to join? A four-year course will soon be eight years with an extra year to deal with carryovers!"

"Hmmm. Sister Jummai, perhaps the students have the right to demand improved facilities and a better learning environment."

"Yes, they do, Prof, but they won't get those things! This is Nigeria. They should stop dreaming."

You could hear the conversation from your room, so you

turned to TikTok videos of post-surgery recovery tips until your eyes gave way to sleep. So you didn't tell them that night either.

Then your father died.

Your father's burial ceremony was scheduled to be a three-day event. On the first day, strange, noisy relatives arrived in hordes and filled your three-bedroom bungalow on Road Seven at the university staff quarters. All dressed in black, the association of wailing aunties was the loudest, occasionally hitting high notes.

"Titó ooooo. Titó has left us. Our only brother!" As the day dissolved into evening, they put their bags in the corner of the living room.

"Témì, please take us to where we will sleep. It is good we are staying here. We need to feed you. You are so slim—you need to chop up."

"Ma?"

Màámi waded in. "I am sure she is excited to eat your food, so she can put on weight. Témì, go and drop their bags in your room." Her eyes pleaded with you to keep quiet.

Later that evening, as you folded your clothes in Màámi's bedroom, you challenged her. "Màámi, why can't these people stay in hotels? Why are we all packed in here like sardines?"

"Témì, your mouth is too sharp. They are family."

"Family members whose names you don't know?"

"Please, go and help Aunty Jummai in the kitchen and let me be."

Your home felt like a face-me-I-face-you apartment with really loud neighbours. The two toilets were always in use. You ended up going over to Ṣọlá's house to relieve yourself. He seemed to take your using his restroom as an invitation to bombard you with solicitous text messages.

> **Hey Témì, I am really sorry about your dad.**
> **Please feel free to come to my house to chill.**
> **We can stay in my room, doing nothing.**
> **. . .**
> **By the way, this is Ṣọlá, your neighbour,**
> **in case you didn't save my number.**

You took him up on his invite, and his room became your hideout. After two days of lying side by side in awkward silence, hopping from one social media platform to another, you asked him to show you how to French kiss. Who knew kissing involved so much saliva? "Ṣọlá, whatever you do, don't touch my breasts!"

"I know all this is trauma bonding, but if you ever feel like taking this further—" he whispered against your lips.

"Ṣọlá, please shut up," you cut in. "You know I don't mess with quarters boys. Who is taking what further with you? Please, let us focus. Kiss me. I want to try biting."

The second day of the burial ceremony was the hardest. You stood between your sister and your mother when they lowered your father into the ground. You saw tears trickle down Ládùn's cheeks onto her bùbù, and your mother just kept muttering your father's name. Didn't they know your father was always going to be around? Just not in physical form.

Later that day, you were in charge of topping up the firewood for the caterers and the aunties who had joined them. You listened to the family gossip they shared with one another, forgetting that you were seated in a corner, avoiding the smoke from the stove. You discovered many things that day.

Apparently, your mother was not the woman your father was supposed to marry, but the moment he met your mother, he forgot about the other woman.

"The woman he jilted refused to marry anyone else. She had hoped that Tító would eventually come back to her. It is her Ẹlẹ́da that is avenging her by killing him. I heard he didn't even go anywhere—Covid just walked in and sat in his body gbam."

"That poor woman," another aunt chimed in. "I send her wishes and prayers at the start of every month because I was the one that introduced them. I feel responsible for her spinsterhood." She blew on the piece of ram she had taken from the caterer's bowl.

"My dear sister, that other woman can't compare to Hassana. Hassana is beautiful. That other woman's teeth alone! Have you seen the arrangement? That woman needs a dentist, not a professor."

"Let us leave that matter. Please, have you seen Lara?"

Your ears stood at attention at the mention of Big Mummy. You were more than interested in hearing your aunt's backstory, and the tidbits were coming hard and fast.

"Her skin looks like it is going through a midlife crisis."

"My dear, the bleaching that woman does is abnormal!"

"Have you seen that small boy she calls her husband?"

"When Titó married that Hausa woman, he abandoned his family."

"God only knows what they gave him to eat. It's as if he forgot he was someone's big brother."

"With nobody to control Lara, she has just been going from man to man."

You did not get much sleep that night because you were sharing your room with Ìyá Ámúsà, who was the last of the guests to leave. Just when you thought she couldn't snore any louder, she increased the volume. You sighed and went over to Ṣọlá's place, where he offered you some edibles.

"I know you like to appear tough, Témì, but your dad's death hit every one of us. So just let it out. Udoka's cookies are legendary." Ṣọlá bit into one of the cookies and held out another.

"How that guy runs a whole weed business from his parents' boys' quarters without their knowledge amazes me," you said.

"He is cashing out big-time! He sells online. I buy from him on Snapchat. You just send him a private message, and he sends one of his delivery guys," Ṣọlá said.

"You know I don't like that stuff. Besides, we have a big day tomorrow. My father's lawyer is coming to read the will."

"This will help, I promise."

You ate the cookies because they were delicious. After that, you began another kissing session. He sucked your tongue like he was hungry, and you nibbled gently on his lips, taking intermittent breaks to catch your breath. Soon, you both lost track of time.

It was Aunty Jummai's voice that woke you at daybreak. "Témì! Food is ready! Come and eat!"

"I have to go," you said, wiping the sleep from your eyes.

"Do you want to go out for ice cream later?"

"No, Solá. My father just died. Ice cream is the last thing on my mind." You saw his face fall, so you quickly added, "Thank you, though. See you tomorrow."

"Sure thing. Sorry." His voice sounded hollow, and his head grew bigger.

You stopped in the doorway to lean on the frame. "Solá, this thing you gave me, is it strong?"

"Nah. You only had three cookies. You will be fine."

As you walked home, your house receded farther into the distance. You picked up your pace until you reached the kitchen door.

"You didn't hear me calling you?" Aunty Jummai demanded as she stood in the kitchen, holding your plate out to you. Was that custard and moin-moin or oats with àkàrà? Everything looked blurry.

"Take it from my hand now. If you are going to be playing cat and mouse with your food as usual, please just leave it. There are too many mouths to feed," she said pointedly.

"Thank you, ma."

"I know you won't listen. Why do I even bother? Coconut head." She shook her head.

"Thank you, Aunty."

You stopped at the dining area to do exactly what she had warned you not to do.

By the time you disappeared into the privacy of your bedroom, different versions of you emerged from the shadows. You felt like you were in that *Matrix* movie your father loved.

"Keanu Reeves is a gem, I tell you. He is like our Richard Mofe-Damijo—both of them gems! Those guys," he would say during family movie night.

"My love, please be quiet. I still don't understand this film." Your mother would shush him so you could all watch the movie for the hundredth time, the entire family cozied up on the sofa.

Focus, Témì! When are you telling them? A version of you who was sitting at the end of the bed interrupted your thoughts.

"I am going to tell them tomorrow!" you replied.

Why would you tell them at all? Màámi will lose it, said another you who was leaning against the door.

Tell them! Tell them! The other three versions of you, who were scattered across the room, egged you on.

"Témì! Please come out, the lawyer is here." Màámi's voice interrupted your conversation.

You headed to the living room, hearing voices. A spicy aroma from the kitchen teased your nose. As you floated down the corridor, you felt happier than you had been in the last fourteen days since your father died. Your mother must have arranged for the reading to happen immediately after the internment. She knew Ládùn could take off at any time.

You sat and watched as Big Mummy, Màámi, Ládùn, and Aunty Jummai listened to the lawyer read your father's will. It felt like everyone else was floating too.

The living room, the same living room where your father had

danced with you so many times, was filled with faces that were worn from tears and despair.

"I will show you that I can still boogie," he always boasted.

"Daddy, nobody says 'boogie' anymore."

"Ahh, sorry. I will show you I am a stepper," he would respond as he zigzagged through the air, throwing his arms everywhere, a move that never failed to make Màámi and Ládùn burst into fits of laughter.

BARRISTER CHIMA STARTED ON A SOLEMN NOTE. "GOOD MORNING. Once again, I am sorry for your loss. No matter what is read today, please know that Tító loved you all so much. He asked me to say this—"

"Lawyer, we know he loved us. Please, let us move fast; you know I am staying in town." Big Mummy pointed her talons toward the door, as if town was a place too far away to describe.

"Please, let him speak," Aunty Jummai said.

The two women looked at each other, each picking the other person up with her eyes and slamming her onto the ground.

The lawyer cleared his throat loudly, his Adam's apple bobbing up and down. You wanted to walk over and touch it to make it stop. His forehead suddenly looked too large. Perhaps he should have considered surgery himself. Forehead surgery.

He began to list everything your father had acquired in his lifetime. He left his house in Ìgboyà, five million naira, the car, and some of his clothes to your mother. He left two million naira, his farm, and some of his books to your sister. He left you the rest of his books, and the guinea brocade shirts you always borrowed, and one million naira. To Aunty Jummai, he left five hundred thousand naira. As the lawyer kept reading, your mother stole glances at Ládùn, and Aunty Jummai sniggered at Big Mummy, as if to say, *After everything, he left you nothing!*

"And that is it. As you know, Prof wasn't the richest man. He was a public servant. However, he made some investments in agritech, and we are hopeful that they will yield returns, which he also willed to your mother." The lawyer put the document back into the folder. His left hand shook, showing his nervousness.

"Wow, wow, wow, Màámi, your husband loved you *o*." You had meant this to be a private thought, but from the wary eyes that immediately looked back at you, you realised you had spoken out loud.

"Thank you all for honouring your father's memory," Màámi stated at a high pitch, as if she had just sucked air from a helium balloon.

Barrister Chima, who everyone knew was waiting for the jollof rice, busied himself with shuffling his files as though he was about to leave.

"Lawyer, don't go yet, please. Let me pack something for you to take away," Aunty Jummai said.

"Your father would have been happy to see us together as a family. So, girls, what are your plans?" Màámi continued.

Silence.

"I am not sure," Ládùn said quietly.

"I assume you are not staying to monitor the farm your father left you."

"Mum, I am sure you are more than capable of sorting that out."

"Farming was you and your father's way of bonding. I know nothing about it."

"He is dead, and I can't do it alone. There are people who actually want this, so please give it to them."

You looked at Ládùn. Her hands were clutching her bag as if she was waiting on an alarm so she could escape.

"What about the house in Ìgboyà?" Màámi asked softly, afraid that Ládùn's next answer might cut even deeper. "I can't look after it by myself."

"Mum, please, you can manage the tenants. If the house needs renovating, we can always discuss that. Let's talk about this later. I am still around for a while."

"Oh, I thought you were leaving after this. No problem, then." Your mother and your sister both looked in different directions.

Big Mummy was staring at her talons, evidently not pleased that her brother had left her out of his will. Aunty Jummai was tapping her feet, probably thanking God for the money your father had left her. The lawyer had started packing his papers into the bag but was being deliberately slow. Everyone's minds had wandered away from the meeting. You figured you might as well just tell them now that they were sombre, so your mother could deal with the pain in one go. You decided the meeting was the perfect opportunity to kill two birds with one stone.

It was either this or send it in the family WhatsApp group, which had been created two weeks earlier and had already become Aunty Jummai's favourite place to send Bible verses, long broadcast audio/video messages, and badly angled, blurry pictures.

You decided to just say it.

Ládùn didn't look at you, but you saw the way her narrow nose twitched and her nostrils flared, which convinced you she had heard. *Good. Now we can all see that everyone in this family can be mad.*

"I don't understand. Is there an injury on your bumbum?" Màámi asked with genuine concern. "Why didn't you tell me, my dear?"

Ládùn's shoulders shook slightly.

"No, Màámi, I am going to get myself a bumbum, like that woman on TV that you always talk about."

"All the women on TV now have big bumbum, Témì. Be straight, please."

"I am going to get a Brazilian butt lift."

"A what? You are going to Brazil?"

"I am adding fat to my buttocks, Màámi."

"I still don't understand! What is wrong with your bumbum exactly?" Màámi asked, looking puzzled.

"It is flat!" you said.

"Was it big before?"

"No, that's why I am going to enlarge it."

Màámi started laughing, but the lines of grief on her face became more pronounced. "Témì, please, this is not the right time to crack jokes. What does your bumbum have to do with your father's death?"

"Màámi, you are the one who asked about our plans—"

Your mother raised her hand. "Témì, please, if you are having a hard time coping with your father's death, I can understand that. You can take a holiday to Lagos. But you are not moving to Lagos, nor are you doing whatever to your buttocks."

"It is not really your decision to make, Màámi. I am an adult."

There was a sinister look on Màámi's face that you had never seen before. She looked up to the ceiling as if to summon your dead father to restrain her from dashing across the room to strangle you.

"You don't know what you are talking about, Témì." Ládùn finally spoke.

"Were you not twenty when you decided to leave the house and never return? *I* am almost twenty-one!"

"We are not talking about your sister, please!" Aunty Jummai cut in.

"Why shouldn't we? She's sitting here, acting like she hasn't been away for five years." Ládùn's eyes met yours. Your recent car conversations came to mind, and you felt yourself thaw.

"Témì, your father has not even been in the ground for a day, and you are already showing your true colours," Aunty Jummai said.

Màámi turned to face you. "Témì, do you want to kill me? You want me to join your father so soon?"

Big Mummy seemed pleased that karma was already biting her brother in the ass. "Let me be on my way. This seems like a private family matter." She inched her frame to the edge of the seat.

"Ahn ahn! Big Mummy, you are their mother as well. You are part of this conversation." Màámi clutched her sister-in-law's arm and turned back to you. "Young lady, who do you even know in Lagos? Where will you stay?"

"I was working my way up to it, Màámi." You turned to your sister. "Ládùn, this is why I wanted to come to your place. Please, can I stay with you in Lagos?"

"Témì, shut your small mouth," Big Mummy interjected.

Aunty Jummai suddenly found her voice again. "Is this what that friend of yours did? That one that came to the burial with the big yansh that did not rhyme with her body. Is it because we didn't disgrace her?"

"Jummai, please wait, is that what her friend did?" Màámi wanted to know, still struggling to make sense of your announcement.

"It must be! Did you not see how her yansh shot out like a misfired bullet?"

"Ah! I thought she had put on weight. Témì, is that what you want to look like?" Màámi asked quietly.

"Jesus! Why our family?" Aunty Jummai clapped her hands and screamed.

Barrister Chima chipped in. "Témì, it is possible that there are legal restrictions on a girl your age going under the knife. I must investigate this." The long-awaited jollof rice was no longer a sufficient reason to remain in the middle of the family commotion.

"Témì wants me to join her father! She wants to kill me!" Your mother leaned on the right arm of your father's favourite chair.

Big Mummy yanked off her head tie and flung it across the room, then ran to pick it up immediately. She circled the sofa, screaming, "La ilaha illallah! They have got Témì! They have got her!"

"Let's look at all the women seated here," you started.

They all looked at one another; only Ládùn looked straight ahead.

You continued. "I can't help but wonder whether it is people from your family that cast a spell on me, Màámi. Why did they not do the same to Ládùn? You all have big butts. I am the only one in the family with a tiny behind. I am going to fix it. I was going to ask you for money to add to my savings because I need compression garments—they call them fája—but I guess from your reaction that none of you will be willing to assist."

They looked increasingly shocked as you spoke; the silence was palpable. The ceiling fan was suddenly louder than the voices in your head. "Aunty Jummai, the rice you are cooking is burning," you blurted out.

As if on cue, Aunty Jummai started crying while Big Mummy gathered her things and hurried toward the door. Màámi sat staring at you while Ládùn looked as though she wanted to be a fly on the wall in a different house. She really had become a stranger.

The harmattan in Ilé-Ifè was still raging that night, although it was late February. As you drowsily searched for the blanket you had kicked off while you slept, you caught a glimpse of your mother, who was sitting at the edge of the bed. Why did Màámi look like she had two heads and four necks? That Udoka deserved a special place in hell.

Màámi had a habit of bending over you at night, either in prayer or tending to you when you were sick. She had started doing it after Ládùn left. She wasn't a religious person, but she began praying for her children and husband. Then, when your father fell sick, she switched to fervent midnight prayers.

"God can hear me better when most people are sleeping. Besides, Jummai's prayers begin at three a.m., and I have to finish before she begins the war with her enemies."

"Màámi!" Your raspy voice made her jerk upright. She looked at you and sighed. There were heavy bags under her eyes.

"Témì, what is wrong with your bumbum? You can tell me. I am a woman like you. I can help."

"Hmmm . . ." You rubbed your eyes, hoping to chase sleep away, then rested your head on your other hand.

"Why would you say you are moving to Lagos and fixing your bumbum?"

"I am not leaving permanently. I just want to see Lagos. Màámi, you came here because you fell in love with Daddy. What if my destiny is in Lagos?"

"With a new bumbum?" Her voice shook a little. "You realise this won't draw men to you? Is that what this is about?"

"No. I am doing it for me."

"Isn't that what killed Stella Obásanjó? She went under the knife and died. So you want me to lose my husband and then lose my child?"

"Màámi, medical science has evolved. I have done the research. The doctor comes highly recommended, and the patients he has operated on have been just fine."

"Where will you get the money?"

"I have savings."

"How much?"

"Errr . . ." you stuttered.

"Témì, how much?"

"Almost two million naira."

"Ahhh! Did you steal it?"

"No, Màámi, I have been saving for a while—and you know I sell hair extensions. Aunty Jummai helped me to start that business at the beginning of the pandemic."

"My dear, I was there when Jummai gave you that money. So you started a hair business so that you can have funds to fix your buttocks. What a wonder!"

"Màámi, please try to understand. I would appreciate it if you could assist me with some extra money to help me survive in Lagos."

"So I should give you money to go and kill yourself?"

"I need money for post-recovery care. I will have to buy some undergarments."

"Témì, I don't understand this. What am I missing? Are you angry with me?"

"Màámi, this is not about you. I would have added breast enlargement to my quest, but thankfully, I have boobs."

"My dear daughter, it is very much about me. I am your mother; every decision you take affects me."

You wondered if you should ask her why she didn't talk Ládùn out of leaving, but you decided not to. "No. It is about me alone."

"You are not coping well with your father's death. There is no other explanation for this," she said. "What about NYSC? Are you not planning to serve your country as expected? You know no one will employ you if you don't finish that first. Is it during your service year that you will be fixing your bumbum? Ehn? While you are teaching or working in a village?" As she continued, the second head on her shoulder started to look like your father. *Who asked you to eat those cookies?*

"Màámi, I will be done with my surgery soon. You know all the non-academic staff are on strike again. The government will waste their time for a few months, pretending they will cave, then the staff will go back to work. I have enough time to do it and re-cover. I will probably be called up with the Batch C."

"Témì the Wise. You have it all figured out. Go to sleep."

"Good night, Màámi."

"Good night."

As she closed the door, you thought of how you would cope with the reality of your father's demise. But you had dealt with Ládùn's mysterious disappearance five years before, and you would deal with your father's death as well, after fixing your bumbum.

LÁDÙN, THE OUTSIDER

I left for the peace and quiet of my hotel room as soon as Aunty Jummai and Big Mummy started their drama. I watched Témì stare at me as we drove off. *Shit. She is not even twenty-one, and she already wants to ruin her life. Who is this girl, and what has she done with my sister?*

Three weeks ago, I was at the club with Ego, the only friend I had in Lagos after Àdùnní left. I enjoyed Ego's company because she was not the type to tell her husband everything, which made it easier to confide in her.

"Ládùn, my husband doesn't know I am aware he is wooing the girl on a nearby street. Just imagine that. We are barely a year into our marriage, and his eyes are already wandering," Ego said.

"I am sorry, Ego." I wanted to hold her hand, but she swatted a fly away from the beer glass.

"Don't be sorry for me; be sorry for him. I am travelling to London in three weeks, and I am going to max out his credit card. Na man wey get money fit toast babe," Ego responded.

The pungent smoke from the súyà spot, mixed with the smell of gin and gathered humans, pervaded the club. Her eyes glistened, betraying the pain she was trying to hide. I was hiding my own pain. It turned out that the man I was in love with was not the person I thought he was, and I needed to get as far away from him as possible. I wanted to ask Ego to pick up my things from Edache's house. I just didn't know what reason to give her.

I looked around the walls, which were plastered with black-and-white patterns. The VIP area and the bar where Àdùnní and I had often sat to count our tips was still separated by strings of multicoloured beads. Blue-and-red lights danced around the ne-glected turntable. "Not much has changed since we worked here," I said, hoping the change in subject would distract her.

"Haba Ládùn, a lot has changed. First, now that the lockdown is over, everyone wants to be out having fun. Also, can you not see all this fake yansh moving up and down?"

"Which fake yansh, Ego?"

"You want to act like you don't know that everybody dey buy bumbum now?"

I stared at the women thronging in and out of the bar with their newly enlarged buttocks. Some looked like follow come, while the states of other behinds suggested the doctors were high on cheap drugs during the surgeries.

"Ládùn, can you see that?" Ego pointed at a woman in a tight-fitting red gown. "That one did her buttocks."

"Ego, how do you know? It looks like she was born with it."

"Born with what, gini? Bia, that one got hers from a doctor I know. She did it last year. Remember that doctor who was widely reported in blogs as the miracle worker?"

"Yes?"

"Exactly! The doctor who did it for her is my friend, and she just relocated to Canada!"

"Wait, why are all the doctors we have in the country relocating?"

"My dear, we only have native doctors left. If you want premium medical care, you have to travel out of this country because—"

"Ma, we don't have Long Island iced tea," a waitress interrupted her.

"Please bring me a stout," Ego replied.

"Which one? Big or small?"

"Small!"

As the waitress walked away, my eyes followed Ego's, which stayed glued to the woman's backside. "Ládùn, that waitress just did her buttocks!" she whispered excitedly.

"You are now the bumbum police, abi?" I traced the geometric patterns on my table mat. "As long as no one I know does it, I am minding my own business."

My father's death brought about the inevitable journey back home. A new wave of sadness blew over me. I was grieving the loss of my father, the loss of my mother's care and my sister's love. It had been five years of finding my way without my family. Five years of becoming. My father came to visit me in Lagos from time to time. However, I never saw my mother. I barely spoke to her or Témì.

The thought of returning home made me shiver. I planned my trip for a late-night arrival, when I reckoned that there would be fewer probing eyes. Ego sent me her driver and her car, and we left at four p.m. the next day. On my way, I marvelled at the slow pace of work on the Lagos-Ìbàdàn Expressway. As the car drove past Òdùduwà University, I felt my heart skip a beat. The familiar smell of àkàrà and fresh bread hawked by vendors wafted through the air as I wound down the window. A billboard with my father's face plastered on it announced his passing and commiserated with the family. My father would have hated the display, but he would have accepted it nonetheless—a trait I wish I had inherited. "We must learn to accept people and their excesses. This is why your aunty Jummai and I never have issues," he said one evening after I complained about Aunty Jummai's loud prayers filtering into the bedroom I shared with Témì.

"Okay, Daddy," I consented.

"Thank you, my first fruit." His smile deepened at the sides, showing his butter-coloured teeth.

THE CAR TIRE SANK INTO A HUGE POTHOLE, AND I KNEW THAT WE were close to the university campus. Once I had checked into the room I'd booked at the university conference centre, I texted Témì so she would know I was on my way. As we drove through Staff Quarters Road, the bungalows were laid out in straight lines. Beds of flowers separated them, and they all looked alike. The only way to know the difference was by the cars parked in front of each house. The branches of the agbalumo tree that had inspired so many of our childhood games littered the road with fruit. *Why did it take me so long to come home?*

When I walked through the front door, open shock was plastered on the faces of the sympathisers. Big Mummy sat on a bench in the corner of the living room, gawking at me, but I just looked on. *I prefer to avoid witches, abeg.* After what she did to Témì and me when we visited her, I had no tolerance for elders without wisdom!

Twelve years ago, Témì and I had to go with Big Mummy to a convention. She was on a quest for a husband at the time. There were rumours in the family that her first husband refused to come back to Nigeria with her, so they got divorced. No one knew if she had children, as she never spoke of any. Our parents had both travelled to Warri for a lecture, so we went to her house in the heart of Ilé-Ifè.

"We are going to have so much fun, my children." She hugged us tight as our mother dropped us off. The three of us waved as she drove away.

"We are taking a little road trip to Iléshà," Big Mummy announced a few minutes later.

"Yayyy! Road trip!" I thought it was like the usual trips we took with our parents. I was wrong.

"Girls, you will eat in two days' time. I promise I will make you delicious àkàrà. For now, you're going to fast with Big Mummy." We spent three days at the convention without eating a bite. Témì and I nearly passed out from hunger. We didn't want Big Mummy reporting us to our parents for not obeying her rules, so we persevered.

"Témì, when she is sleeping, we will sneak out to go and look for food. I have some money. We have forty minutes, so eat all you can, and remember we have to run back before she wakes up," I whispered as the midday service ended on the fourth day. As soon as Big Mummy dozed off, we snuck out into the streets and ended up finding a great spot where the sign announced that they sold freshly pounded yam and goat meat.

"This food is so delicious, Témì." I watched as my sister demolished the mountain of iyán, catching the leaking oil from the ègúsí with her tongue. I imitated her speed.

"Sister mi, even Màámi can't cook like this."

"Aaaah! Don't say that."

"What is going on here?" We both looked up to see the prayer leader towering over Témì. "Are you not Ms. Tóyèbí's kids?"

Without thinking, Témì and I bolted, oil dripping all over our clothes, laughter bursting from our lips. "It is good we had paid for our meals before eating."

"Let's hope he doesn't find us or Big Mummy during the service. Kneel and let us pray," I whispered as soon as we snuck back into the church quarters.

Big Mummy stood by the door. "Where are you two coming from?"

Témì and I held hands. The oil had stained our dresses. My eyes followed Big Mummy's downward gaze. "So you and your spirits are now so tied to food that you can't go without it for a mere three days?" I was quiet.

We spent the last day at the convention reciting a poem.

I will not go to hellfire if I follow Jesus
Food and drinks belong to the world
If I follow them, I am going to hellfire
Enjoyment belongs to the world
If I follow it, I am going to hellfire

Big Mummy drove home in silence, and we didn't eat that evening.

"You are spoilt children. Your parents won't listen to me. They should send you to live with me. Go to bed!" she said as she picked beans from the plastic tray sitting unevenly on her thighs. The aroma of beans and dodo tortured us throughout the night. Our stomachs rumbled, so we told each other stories until the break of dawn. The next day, our father came to pick us up.

He swung me around, thanked his sister, and drove off. "My jolly girls, I have missed you. Did you have fun with your Big Mummy?"

I shrugged.

"How was it?" he asked again, this time with a note of seriousness in his voice.

"It was fine." He looked at me through the rearview mirror. He drove to Ìbàdàn first. He took us to Cocoa House, one of our favourite places. We ate mouthwatering shrimps and peppered snails, and drank Coca-Cola.

"I don't even want to know what happened. I am sorry, and I promise you will never go back there."

In the evening, as we drove into the staff quarters, singing along to songs playing on the radio, Màámi stood in the garden with a woman who looked very much like her, but an angry, shorter version. That was the day Aunty Jummai moved in.

I caught Aunty Jummai looking at me with fear in her eyes. *Yes, be very afraid!*

I noticed there was a look of longing on my mother's face and an absent expression on Témì's. I ignored my mother, but with Témì, I felt something was amiss. I greeted every family member individually, watching them judge me. *Yes, yes, the black sheep has returned—abeg free me.* I sat at the dining table. An hour later, Témì finally acknowledged my presence and walked over, fiddling with the hem of her dress. After what seemed like an eternity, she pulled out a chair and sat beside me.

She placed her phone on the table between us. "Daddy said I should play this for you." The video opened with my father in bed, the camera so close that I could see the hairs in his nose. Témì suddenly zoomed out, this time capturing the droopy skin on my father's oval face. I caught a glimpse of the yellow bottle of pills on his bedside table.

"I know my recording is not great," Témì mumbled.

"No, it's great! I love it. I can see his face and everything," I whispered.

My father looked peaceful but weak, and when he reached out to touch Témì, the camera shook slightly. He started praying. "May you and your sister find joy. May the earth welcome you every-where you go and favour you. May you always remember to be friends. May your homes be filled with laughter. Your husbands will like each other. Your children will be friends. You will be celebrated."

I heard Témì say, "Amen," quietly. It felt like someone was tearing my right arm from my body. I fell apart; I cried for both of them. And myself. For the moments I had missed because my anger had been stronger than my love.

I AVOIDED NOSY RELATIVES BY STAYING IN MY HOTEL ROOM AND only coming to the house for the main events each day. Témì escorted me to my car every night. She showed me more videos and pictures of our father.

"Témì, you know you can come stay with me at the conference centre if the house is too full," I told her the night I arrived.

"Màámi won't let me sleep over. She says the conference centre is not safe." She stared at her reflection on the car.

"I am surprised she even let you follow me to the car alone, in case I corrupt you with my Lagos mind."

"No, it's cool," she said. She bit her lower lip before she spoke again. "Ládùn, I have been meaning to ask you, can I come stay with you in Lagos?"

"Will Màámi let you?"

"She will. Just for a little while."

"Let's talk about it later." I hoped she would forget about it.

Throughout the burial rites, Témì never cried once, as if she believed our father would return someday.

The will reading showed that Témì was not doing okay at all. Where was my father when I needed him the most? He knew how to handle tricky situations. He was always there at crucial moments in my teenage years.

One afternoon, during the school's compulsory siesta, I felt a searing pain in my lower belly, so I approached the headmistress for permission to go home.

"Ládùn, your parents are not answering the phone. I have called and left messages. Do you want someone to drop you off?"

"No, ma. I can find my way home."

She gave me the permission slip. As I was about to alight from the bus close to the staff quarters, an elderly woman whispered, "Sisí, there is a bloodstain at the back of your skirt. Go home quickly and change."

"Thank you, ma."

The insides of my thighs were warm and sticky. My lower belly felt like fingers with long talons were pinching it. I was afraid my blood would trickle down my legs and form a trail on the gravelled road. My father was stepping out as I walked into our compound. "My first fruit, why are you home?"

"I was about to ask you the same question."

"I forgot the textbook I want to share with some of my postgraduate students. What's wrong?"

"I am in pain, Daddy. There is blood everywhere." I showed him the back of my pinafore.

"Sweetheart, is this the first time this is happening?"

"Yes, sir."

"Makes me wonder what they teach you in that school of yours if they have not enlightened you on what this is about. Come, sweetie. Go and shower; I'll get you a sanitary pad. I'll leave painkillers on the table for you too. Do you want me to boil some water for you to drink? I hear it helps."

"Thank you, Daddy. I'm willing to try anything."

When my mother got home, she made pepper soup for me.

"Pèlé, Ládùn. Your father said he has already spoken to you. I'll show you some things when you feel better."

"Ládùn, e pèlé. Màámi said you are seeing blood. What is wrong?" Témì asked me.

Before I could answer, we both heard Màámi's voice. "Témì, is that what I told you? Leave your sister alone!"

I lowered my voice and told Témì what was happening, to keep her from pestering me.

She gasped. "Ah, so you mean this same thing will happen to me?"

"No. We are different."

"No, we are not. We are sisters."

"I mean your own menstrual period will arrive without pain. You are too beautiful for pain, Témì."

"Ládùn!" She smiled warmly and hugged me.

"Just make sure you go to the sick bay and ask for pads whenever it comes," I told her.

"I will."

"Good girl. Mummy gave me two hundred naira. Let's go and buy ice cream."

The memories came flooding back. Was my life in Lagos so hectic that I had become self-absorbed? How could I have let my anger toward Mummy make me miss my father's last days?

Two weeks before he passed, Daddy had sent a text:

My first fruit, your father is a little weak. I will see you next week. Greet Edache for me. I hope you have finally found a way to tell him about us. I can't wait for you to come home. Till next time. I love you.

I responded swiftly:

Okay, old man. I love you so much.

And he replied:

Not as much as I love you, child of my youth. We will go to Ìbàdàn for àmàlà before we go home. My treat.

Those were his last words to me—a text message. I didn't get a chance to say a proper goodbye.

Now Témì wants to go to Lagos, the place I am running from and hoping to avoid for many years.

Fuck Covid-19 and everything it has brought to me!

HASSANA'S WOMB

Mama didn't live to see any of her grandchildren, but she left enough wisdom to guide me. "You must straighten their noses, shape the girls' backsides, and give their heads a good shape. Don't let your child's head look like a box, Hassana." Yet I neglected to shape Témì's buttocks. I didn't touch Ládùn's either, but she took after my mother—shapely like a Coca-Cola bottle. My mother birthed seven children, but five of them died mysteriously before their first birthday. I was the only one who stayed, until Jummai came along. "You, my beautiful Hassana, you fought the evil powers of your father's people that sent the disease to take my children. Your twin didn't fight as hard, but you did. You are the reason I have you and Jummai." Mama never failed to mention whenever I did anything that pleased her—something Jummai rarely achieved.

Jummai has always had a big mouth, especially when it comes to other people's matters. She enjoys making my children look bad so that no one will remember that her own children see her only once a year. The shameless woman is having an affair. She thinks I don't know. She now does her hair every two weeks, the smell of sulphur hair cream constantly mixing with the aroma of our meals. Her high shuku enters the room before the rest of her, trailed by strong, musky perfume. Her latest distraction must reside in town because she is always out and about.

Big Mummy, on the other hand, is a hypocrite who assumes I don't know what she did to my children when they visited her. Why would anyone punish children with compulsory fasting? She may not like me, but I know she would do anything to ensure that the family name is not tarnished. She will help me with this Témì wahala.

I can't believe Témì wants to go under the knife at this age. Does she not know that a woman's body constantly changes and loses its elasticity? What will she do when she gives birth? Has she experienced the way the vagina tears open, and for days, it feels like there is an unzipped fly between your legs? Maybe then she will reconstruct her entire body.

There are days when I stand and look at my body and wonder where the young woman has gone. Témì makes it seem like she is the first person born with a body part that is a source of worry. I remember after I had her, Big Mummy came into my room one night. "Your breasts are on the ground, Hassana. You are too young to be carrying slippers on your chest." I have had saggy boobs all my life, but that night, I wished my body was different. But we must all be stronger than the words people throw at us; otherwise, we never move forward.

"Don't mind her—you are the sexiest woman in every room. She is just insensitive," Titó reassured me when I reported the incident to him. I believed him because he never lied to me. I was beautiful because Titó told me so and showed me so.

Later that day, I heard him say to her, "Lara, please don't talk to Hassana in a condescending manner. She is my wife. If you disrespect her, you disrespect me."

"So, Titó, your wife is above me?"

"Yes, she is."

That night, I gave him a bath, and then I rode him like I had read in those *Hints* magazines.

"Hassana, you want to kill me?" he kept panting as I squeezed him with my walls. We peaked together, and I was certain she heard us from the guest room.

Témì might say it is not about validation, but I am certain she is not doing this for herself. I can't even raise two girls right. Oh, my poor baby, Témì! How did I miss it? How did I miss the signs that my baby was unhappy with her body? The jokes we made during family gatherings were never in poor taste, abi was I just not listening enough? I have already failed Ládùn, and now Témì, who I had hoped would cover my shame, has decided to expose me.

Ládùn has been around for a week, but she is lodging at the conference centre. I know this because Dr. Anyadike mentioned he had seen her there.

"Hassana, why is Ládùn at the conference centre? I saw her there two nights ago, and the receptionist confirmed she is staying there." His right eyebrow lifted, and he bent his head toward me as if he could see the answer in my eyes, if he stared hard enough.

"You know how these children can be when they are older. She says the house is too busy and she needs her own space," I lied, looking at his wrinkled shirt collar.

I can't seem to find any time to be alone with her, and the girl won't even look at me. When she sees me coming, she heads in the opposite direction, as if I have leprosy. A child I carried in my belly for ten months!

Her cheeks look like freshly fried puff-puff, her eyes are surrounded by light shadows, and her ankles look like there is water hidden under them and it keeps dancing as she moves. I hope she is not pregnant. I would be very upset with her if she did that to me.

A WEEK BEFORE HE PASSED AWAY, TITÓ AND I HAD A CONVERSAtion when I brought her up.

"Why is your daughter not here? Why have we not called her to come here? What kind of child does this to her parents?" I said as I prepared his evening bath, beating the overflowing bubbles as if they were Ládùn.

He got into the bath, and after ten minutes of silence, even though my eyes were intently on him, waiting, he spoke slowly, his fingers beating against the bathtub as if his words were guided by imaginary musical bars. "My love, you must understand that our children are a reflection of us, but they are also driving their own lives. Ládùn and I are making headway; things will get better with you two. But, baby, you can't tie these children down to be who you want; just accept their decisions."

"Hmmm. I have heard you. We will let them be who they want."

"Thank you, baby."

That was why when Témì sat before me to tell me she wanted

to go and open up her body with a knife, I wanted to jump up and bite her, but I restrained myself.

Children can be wicked. They wait until they are older before showing you pepper for everything you did wrong in their childhood. Now I am alone because my best friend has left me. My two children would rather go into a city that is likely to swallow them than stay here with me. Why won't children learn? I have seen life. I have been to places that they couldn't imagine. They think I don't hear their jokes.

"Màámi can't leave Ilé-Ifẹ̀. She is stuck."

"I am surprised she goes on vacation with us. I don't know why anyone would love Ilé-Ifẹ̀ this much."

I hear them all.

In my dreams, I thought Titó and I would be together forever, but influenza and high blood pressure were the weapons that death employed to force me back to reality. Titó was a professor of philosophy, yet he was not smart enough to know he had to attend routine checkups. I sat in shock as the doctor gave us the diagnosis. I watched his lips move but could not make out the sounds. My head was pounding. I wanted to plunge my hands into Titó's body and wrench out the illness.

Dr. Anyadike's voice pulled me out of my trance. "Thankfully, your latest test results show that you are now Covid negative. However, Covid has alerted us to other health complications. You should have come in earlier, but we'll try our best. Titó, you are no spring chicken."

Titó smiled, and I wanted to slap him. This was not the time to joke with his best friend. *How dare you fall sick? This was not the agreement!* I felt guilt tugging at my heart for jumping on the bandwagon and rejecting the vaccine. At our last family meeting, we resolved to *just wash our hands, wear face masks, and be careful.* After learning of the diagnosis, Jummai spent three days on the mountain. "I will pray the infection away, Ègbón mi." She brought concoctions from the mountain and invited prophets into our home. Tító knelt between candles while they performed their rituals. "Jésù dìde! Dìde Olùwa!" They moved in circles, gyrating and clapping their hands. I was concerned that Tító would be drenched in sweat and saliva, but sometimes during the prayers, he would wink at me. He read the Bible verses loudly, as instructed by the prophets, his voice belying the weakness of his shaky hands as he thumbed through the chapters, squinting to recite the healing verses. He shook his head vigorously and nodded in agreement when they said they would kill the sickness with spiritual blows. "Thank you, àbúrò," Tító would say, after drinking their concoctions.

He was a better sibling to her than I am. I don't hide the fact that I merely tolerate her. I don't engage with her when she tries to draw me into conversation. I treat her like a familiar stranger.

Tító and my children were the only reminders that the universe liked me. I married a good man. We tried our best as parents. Now these children are going to Lagos; one to fix her bumbum, the other to stay as far from me as possible. Ládùn can think whatever she wants. Let's see how well she does when she becomes a mother. Perhaps we should have had boys.

JUMMAI, THE BIG MOUTH

*I thought most Nigerian men married women for their agree-*able behaviour, cooking skills, and their exaggerated moans as they pounded between their legs, or was that a ruse? Does physical appearance matter? Isn't that what mistresses are for? The wives can be passable in appearance, but the mistresses must be eye candies. Is Témì trying to end up as a mistress?

Some time ago, I read about a musician who was quoted on the internet saying, "A vagina is what a man is really after, every other thing na wash." I slept well that night because I knew that regardless of how important some of those arrogant married women in my church felt, they were nothing but vaginas to their husbands.

It would not have come as a surprise if it was Ládùn who decided to scatter the family with a nonsense announcement. Témì is a good girl. She may not always wear pata, but she is a decent girl. Since her sister left, I have been waiting for her to act out. I watched her bury herself in her friends, but I knew Ládùn's sudden departure took a toll on her. I wanted to save her from the no-good pack that lurked around.

"Why are you always following that Bòbóólá girl around?"

"She is my friend, Aunty."

"She has the eyes of a hawk. I don't trust her."

"Aunty Jummai, Bòbọólá is a good person."

Thankfully, I noticed they stopped being friends a while ago. I hadn't probed. As long as the girl no longer came over to our house, *no wahala.*

I sat Témì down to have a conversation about two years ago. "Témì, now that you are no longer doing follow follow with your friends, and you are in your final year, why not start a business?"

"I don't know anything about business."

"I do. I can give you some tips on how to start selling hair attachments that those wigmakers in your hostel can use for braided wigs. You know I am learning hairdressing, so I have contacts who can supply the attachments."

To my utter surprise, she acquiesced. She simply asked for the capital, and I gave it to her. "I will collect my fifty thousand naira back in six months."

"Okay, Aunty."

I knew the business was doing well because I had to order for her every two months in bulk. I was happy for her. Hassana didn't thank me for investing in her child. Professor was the only one who acknowledged my good deed.

Who is responsible for Témì's madness? Is it that famous girl Joke Rose, or the men who constantly talk about women's bodies as if they are shopping for spare parts at Ládípò market in Lagos? Why would she choose to disgrace us like this? When did bumbum become a big deal? She can take some of mine, because it definitely hasn't given me an edge in life. If it was by backside that men valued us, my husband would still be here.

No! I will chase this spirit out of Témì. This is a project for Prophet Túndé, not my prophets on the mountain. Ever since their visit failed to stave off the professor's death, I stopped believing in their prayers. This demon in Témì is a walk in the park for my dear prophet. I am sure Hassana thinks I will disclose Témì's announcement to our next-door neighbour, Ṣọlá's mother. *Ahn ahn, when I am not possessed!* This is not the kind of news you gossip about. It would scandalise our family and mar our reputation.

Since Ládùn left this house, I have been reading about the behavioural patterns of children like her. I have no doubt that she is possessed. The night she fought with her mother, I tried to persuade her to forgive Hassana. Do you know she drew a knife on me? Me, Jummai?

"Let this be the last time you speak to me that way, Aunty Jummai," Ládùn threatened that night. "And even when I leave this house, if you bother Témì, I will appear in your dreams and kill you!" I gave her space because I didn't know the powers operating in her.

I trust my own children; they would never act like this. Even if that man won't let me see them regularly, I send them Bible chapters every day through WhatsApp, and funny videos too. I also send them messages saying, "I love you," to remind them. They may not respond, but I know they see them. Maybe their father doesn't allow them to chat with me. They came for the burial in the morning and left immediately after the service, as if scared that I would infect them with some disease if they stayed any longer.

Professor loved my sister. Maybe too much. I would have said that she *jazzed* him, but I know she isn't bold enough to do that—she wouldn't even touch the Keep-Your-Husband anointing oil I got from church.

"This is wrong, Jummai. I won't use it," Hassana said, shooing me away.

"Sister mi, they say it will also help you have a son," I pleaded.

"My husband loves me. He loves his daughters."

Their love made no sense. No gìrìgìrì, just *soft soft*. The only time they ever fought was when Ládùn left, and the fight didn't last the night. I heard them making love and him whispering, "I am sorry, my love. I should not have shouted."

"I don't know why she hates me. She is so—" Hassana started crying.

He shushed her, and a few minutes later, the moaning started again.

"My love, take me in," Professor panted.

My ears stayed glued to their door until they started to muffle their sounds. Shameless people! Who fucks after a child leaves the family in disarray?

Now, Témì wants to go and tear herself apart, my dear professor is dead, and my children won't respond to my WhatsApp messages.

What is happening, God? Are you on vacation?

BIG MUMMY IS NOT ANGRY

This is what happens when you spare the rod and spoil the child. I have had my heart broken many times for trying to do the right thing, especially with Témì and that sister of hers. The moment Ègbón brought that ará ìta home, I knew trouble would trail her. He might have been distracted by her beauty, but couldn't he have kept her as his concubine? Why couldn't he marry a Yoruba woman? Témì got her rudeness from her mother. Maybe it is a family trait. Or is it even cultural? Once Allah gives me a baby, I will show these people how to bring up a child properly. Insha'Allah.

I remember when I tried to spank Témì. She was just a child then. I had called out to her several times during a visit to their house. I heard nothing, and then the tiny girl waltzed into the living room, looking like I had interrupted something important.

"Témì, did you not hear me calling you?"

"I was arranging my clothes for school, Big Mummy." Her voice wavered between anger and respect. I was miffed.

"So you could not leave the clothes for two minutes?"

"No, ma! Màámi will be upset with me if my clothes for the week are not properly arranged and ironed."

"Témì, is it me you are talking back to?" I hadn't intended to hit her. I just wanted to scare her. You should have seen the way her parents rushed in when she screamed.

"Lara, please do not lay your hands on my child. We don't condone that here," Ègbón said to me. I couldn't believe my brother was talking to me like that in front of his child.

"Big Mummy, you can just discuss things with her, and she will listen. We try to run a cane-free house," Hassana added.

Cane-free indeed! That silly girl should have been flogged senseless! They made me feel like an infant being scolded by adults for a shameful indiscretion. "E má bínú o," I said. I left that evening and never spent the night there again. It was a shame because I enjoyed my time in the staff quarters. The room I stayed in before they kicked me out for Jummai was decorated with my woven baskets and some of the alari we inherited from our parents. There was a steady supply of power and water, and the security was tight.

I have always tried to raise my brother's children the way I would raise my own, but it is too easy to offend these modern parents. After the church convention where I encouraged the girls to fast and pray, Tító and Hassana refused to bring the children to my house, knowing full well that a spinster needs company to ward off loneliness. Thankfully, I found a husband after that debacle. Subhan Allahi wa bi hamdihi.

I am not angry that my only brother left me out of his will. I am not angry that he did not give me the farm after I dropped several hints that I wanted it. I am not angry that he left his wife's sister something—why should I be angry? Is that not life? Are siblings sometimes not the biggest traitors? I blame our parents.

If they had lined his eyes with atarodo pepper when he went astray, he would not have been so blind to his children's faults. Instead, they carried him like an egg. Now look, the son they didn't train has forgotten to train his own daughters. I was the one who had to be taught everything.

"You are a woman. If you go to your husband's house with this bad character, they will think we did not train you," my mother would often say.

I have always known that Témì would turn out strange. That's what happens when you give your children too much leeway. Any well-brought-up child would know to vacate a room when adults are talking. But not Témì. "Témì, come and sit with us," he would call out to her.

"Ègbón, she is a child."

"I can't leave her by herself. We can still talk; she is a baby. She won't know."

The way her eyes followed me as I described the situation with my new husband, who was a child I found myself catering to day and night, I knew she understood what I was saying. "I am exhausted, Ègbón. I don't know if it is because he is younger. You should see our house—na so-so weed, beer, and yelling at the television whenever his favourite team doesn't win."

"Just be patient with him."

"I don't have a choice. Now he is asking me for children."

Let's not talk even about Ládùn, because one minute she was living in Ilé-Ifè, and the next, they were all pretending they had just one child. Honestly, not every couple should have children. Those two did not do a good job.

Alhamdulillahi, I am not a poor woman. My ex-husband still sends me money—he is my tenant in the UK. When we first met, I let him move in with me because I was young, in love, and foolish. But love wasn't enough to keep me squashed in a two-bedroom flat with his extended family, who came to squat and never left. After two years, I couldn't bear it anymore, and I returned to Nigeria, leaving house and marriage behind.

"A woman must endure," my mother said to me months later. I ignored her. I was happy to be alone after I moved back home, but then my laughter started to echo in the empty house, and I missed human warmth. So I started to dress better. Every night, I drenched myself in palm oil before washing it away with Ọṣẹ Dúdú. Then I rubbed shea butter into my skin. I thought it would only take a few months. How hard is it to find a husband in Ilé-Ifẹ̀? Very hard. Months turned to years. No man.

After growing up with churches and mosques with their noise and morning calls, I dumped religion as soon as I was old enough to make a choice. Any God I did not see was not getting my attention, please. But after many months without a glance or even a whistle from the opposite sex, I had no choice. I turned to prayer, and prayed so hard, my tongue threatened to leave my mouth. I attended revivals, but still nothing. One evening, I was returning from my shop after a good day, having sold over ten cartons of drinks, when I saw that my neighbour down the street was getting married. How had that haggard-looking hijabi found a husband before me? I decided to befriend her. A woman I wouldn't be caught eating with on my hungriest day became my closest friend.

"Lara, I never knew you were this friendly," she said to me one evening as we were eating cow-leg pepper soup. There were strands of beef stuck in her darkened teeth.

"Haba, my Alhaja, I am just a reserved person."

"Which one is reserved?" She laughed. "You are always speaking big, big grammar. Speak Yoruba!" She lifted a foot and gingerly placed it next to my bowl.

"Mo ti gbọ́. As we spend more time together, I will get better, with your guidance."

"Ehn ehn, now you are talking. My dear, we are all looking to Allah for guidance." I resisted the urge to slap her crusty foot off the stool.

"You are looking very nice today, Alhaja. This, your beautiful skin, one could mistake you for a mixed race. Oyinbo pepper." She smiled at my compliment. Dirty woman! Her yellow-green skin was a horrible thing to look at, but her new husband worshipped every inch of it. She had married the mechanic who owned a workshop close to the stadium. The man was a widower, and both his children lived in America. He had packed up all his things and moved into her house. After a few months of my dancing around her like waist beads, one evening, after we had eaten èko and àkàrà, she said to me, "I want to give you a gift, Lara." Shortly after, a man arrived. "This is my Alfa, my leader, the one who sees it all, the one who directs my life," she said.

A bearded man in a dusty white turban bowed and covered his heart with his palm. As he moved toward me, oversized beads on his misbaha stared like tiny eyes. "Your husband is ready for you. Ọkọ ni olórí aya. He is your crown! Kneel and let me place him on your head," he said with gusto.

"Lara, do as he says!" she spoke suddenly.

I first stood transfixed, then I fell to my knees. *How did this man know my heart's desire?*

"Say after me. My husband, come here now!" Alfa shouted.

"My husband, come here now!" I said.

"My husband, my womb is ready for your seed!"

"My husband, my womb is ready for your seed!" My hands clutched my belly.

"My husband, come and claim me!"

"My husband, come and claim me!"

After a long silence, he listed the next steps. "First, you must pray nonstop on the mat for seven days. Number two, when you wake up, take your mouth to the wall, and say these words: 'I call to the north, I call to the south, I call to the east, I call to the west. Anywhere my husband is, even if he has to walk through this wall, he must come and find me.' Thirdly, do not eat meat for three months. If you do, you will be eating your husband's penis. Finally, madam, you are too dark. Good men want light in their homes. Become a light!" That was it. After six months of praying hard and using Fair & White, I found a husband. He came to my store with his girlfriend to buy drinks. "Sister, you and your husband make a beautiful couple," I said. I had to have him.

"We are not married yet, ma." The young woman clasped her fingers together and looked at the floor.

My husband didn't say anything but I knew he could be

snatched by strong hands. His eyes lingered on my flawless face. Finally, somebody was seeing my light. I hid some of the drinks they asked for. "I will have them in stock tomorrow," I said, hoping he would return unaccompanied.

"I can pick up the drinks. That's not a problem at all," the man said. I nearly leapt for joy.

"Are you sure?" the young woman asked. "If madam is okay with it, we can come the day after, since I'll be busy tomorrow."

"I don't mind. I'll come alone."

Exactly, let him come alone, dear.

The next day, I showered him with praise. "You are so handsome, Habibi." I turned to my sales girl. "Bọ́sẹ̀, go and fetch my special wine, please. A worthy guest is here."

When Bọ́sẹ̀ finished filling our glasses, I sent her on a long errand. He didn't speak, but I knew he was looking for a woman to worship him. His eyes gave him away. I sucked, I sucked, and then I swallowed. I showed him what an older woman could do.

Now he is mine. I know they talk about me in the family, and I don't care. A second marriage. At least men marry me.

I received a message from Hassana, inviting me to another meeting so we could discuss Témì's situation further. I wanted to write, "So now my opinion on how to raise children matters? Interesting!" Instead, I wrote, "I will be there, Insha'Allah," because I am not petty.

BARRISTER'S BELLY

Character is like smoke. Words failed Barrister when Témì spoke.
The girl couldn't have chosen a worse time to make such an announcement. She could have waited for them to pack his jollof rice in a takeaway bowl. That is one of the perks of having Yoruba clients—they may kill a person with pepper, but they will fill the belly.

You see, Barrister Chima was already in a bad mood before the reading of the will, because he had just incurred some expenses. Barrister preferred his side chicks to have perky breasts and big backsides, so he'd sent money to his new smallie to get her body done by his good friend, Dr. 90210. What was the point of having extramarital affairs if the women didn't fit your fantasy? Barrister was a simple man with a tamed Afro, growing potbelly, and an insatiable hunger for beautiful women. He encouraged his side chicks to look their sexiest, and if they had to go under the knife for that to happen, so be it. They were adults after all, over twenty-five. They knew what they were getting into. The idea of Témì wanting to play in the big girls' club confused Barrister.

As Barrister scurried out of the Tóyèbí home, his thoughts went to his family. "I hope my daughter doesn't harbour these ideas, because I will kill her before she disgraces me," he mumbled as he got into his car. His wife had no backside, but her brains and eternal gratitude were sufficient for him. She gave him peace, but he sought thrills with his smallies outside, because every man needs balance to function properly. The only thing he never did was bring it home. Even his girls knew better than to seek a future with a happily married man. Everyone was getting what they wanted. Perhaps he was giving more, because he expected the body upgrades to result in them finding more suitable spouses. Of course, he usually paid for the wedding as a send-off gift, but they would fuck one last time—some sort of one-for-the-road ritual.

Nkiru, the one he was with before Obiageli, had a moist mouth and a deep throat. Oh dear Lord, that mouth! When they met, he often didn't even need to fuck her; her mouth was all he needed. Sometimes he slapped the ass he paid for as a reminder that he owned the body she flaunted on social media.

Barrister liked the Tóyèbís. You could tell they were a stable family—a doting husband and a submissive, beautiful wife with two gorgeous daughters. Even Titó's sister-in-law fit nicely into the family. She was a good cook, and not bad-looking either.

Titó had given Barrister some of the money that he used to buy his first car. In his blue Peugeot 504, Barrister blasted Fela songs and drove with his seat reclined and his arm stretched to its full length. Those were good times.

"Chima, take it easy with the girls in this new car," Titó used to say to Barrister whenever he visited.

"My doctor of philosophy, trust me *now*. I am a lover, not a fighter" was his usual response.

Although Titó was older, he had an amiable personality, which made his friendship with Barrister easy. Most times when they hung out, they laughed together as they combed through nightclubs in their bell bottoms, flared shirts, and Afros. Barrister noticed Titó never went home with a girl. He assumed Titó had an uneducated wife whom he was ashamed to bring to the staff club. One day, after the Ifè/Modákéké war ended, they were drinking palm wine at the staff club when Titó walked in with a woman in tow. "Chima, meet my wife, Hassana Tóyèbí."

"Nice to meet you." Barrister took in Hassana's long lashes, brown eyes, and heart-shaped lips. The woman was beautiful, but it was her backside that held Barrister's attention. He felt a stirring, but he crossed his legs. They had a code—no sleeping with your friends' women, present or past. Back then, you could trust your friends, but nowadays, Barrister had to keep reminding his guys to stay away from his smallies.

Titó's death hit Barrister hard. He was unable to go to court for nearly two weeks, assigning all his cases during that period to his junior associate. Now Titó's family was in chaos because of his last child's waywardness. Barrister had not seen Titó's older daughter in a while. He noticed how she sat like a visitor in her own father's house and wondered why. The last time he had seen Ládùn with her father, they were coming from the farm, and the professor dropped off some produce for him. The excitement on Ládùn's face when she told the barrister how her father showed her the proper way to prepare manure made Barrister wish he and his daughter had a similar relationship. Barrister was sure the absence of his child contributed to Tító's death. Maybe it was a guilty conscience that was eating at her. Why would any child not come home for five years?

Barrister's thoughts went back to Témì. He felt sad for her because he knew how pressured young ladies were. The competition was stiff. These girls knew they could buy both body and beauty, so the game was rigged. No one cared about a girl's character; if she could fuck, cook, and keep her mouth shut, she would find a husband. But Témì was not just anyone; she was his friend's daughter. Barrister once ran into Témì when he was out with one of his smallies on Ẹdẹ Road, near the women's hostel. She looked away quickly, as if seeing him with a side chick embarrassed her. The next time he went to their house, she had that wry smile that said, *I know what you have been doing.* He was glad that she didn't mention it to her father.

Tító couldn't stand men who cheated on their wives. "If you want to be a philanderer, don't marry and make your woman believe she is inadequate," he would often say.

"Abeg, Tító, shut up! Go and drink the kùnnú your àbókí wife is feeding you at home," Adéòsun, a linguistics professor, replied drunkenly. That day, for the first time, Barrister Chima saw Tító get angry. He got up, walked out, and then came back in immediately and squared up to Adéòsun. "Never, ever disrespect my wife again! All of you! My family is off-limits!"

As much as Barrister admired Tító, he knew cheating was second nature to man. Barrister rubbed his stomach absentmindedly. He made a mental note to tell his daughter to stay away from that family. He didn't want their madness to infect his children.

part two

YESTERDAY, AND THE BODIES THAT WALKED THROUGH IT

TÉMÌ IS ALSO A MOPSTICK!

You started padding your pants with singlets at the age of ten, but it wasn't because your bumbum was flat. The flatness wasn't your problem; it was the fact that it was also inverted, as though it were afraid to grow. For a long time, you thought your middle name was Lepa Shandy.

You really didn't think anything was wrong with your body until Big Mummy pointed out how thin you were on your eighth birthday. "Hassana, are you not feeding this child?"

"I am *o*. Don't mind her," Màámi said.

"You, this girl, when will you put on weight? Ego ta mọ́ bus. When you come to my house, I will give you plenty of meat."

"Don't worry, she will come," Màámi promised.

You paid no mind to the banter because you knew from looking at your mother and sister, you would eventually be fine. But her words stayed with you.

In Primary 5, you liked a boy called Truth. He had the most beautiful curls you had ever seen. They flowed like a wave from the top of his head down to the nape of his neck, cascading into a single curl that you always wanted to touch. Truth's mother was responsible for his hair—she was part Lebanese, part Nigerian.

You knew all this about him because your classmates told you. You sat with groups of girls on the tree stumps behind your classrooms, listening to every detail.

"He is going to move to Germany after primary school."

"I will follow him because he is my husband."

"I have written him many letters. Even though he doesn't respond, I know he will be mine."

Although you were silent, every word spoken about Truth was engraved in your memory. His uniform was never rumpled; his shirt and shorts were always starched. If there was anyone who could capture the scent "clean" in a bottle and sell it, it was Truth. You had never spoken to him, but in your fantasies, you were married and had two children.

After primary school, during the six-month waiting period for a secondary school to offer you a place, you summoned the courage to introduce yourself, and you became friends. He was also staying in the staff quarters, where you and all the children of your age group found fun activities to keep you busy. On one of those days, Truth walked you and Abigail home, with her newest admirer in tow.

"Imagine if we go to the same schools for the rest of our lives and end up getting married," you said, musing about your future.

Truth scoffed. "That can never happen. Your shape is similar to a mopstick. Lepa Shandy like you. Me that I like big bumbum. Have you not seen my mother?"

The pain in your chest stopped you from asking why he felt so comfortable looking at his mother's ass. Big Mummy's words came rushing back, and you realised something was indeed wrong with your body. You started looking at other girls' buttocks. Was there something they used that you didn't know about? You had to wear all of Ládùn's old clothes once you started secondary school, and that didn't help. "They are too big for me, Màámi. It's not fair!" You flapped your arms in the patterned long-sleeved dress to show how it swallowed you.

"You will grow into them. You know that these clothes are just for wearing at home. Can't you just wear them to make me happy, oko mi?" Màámi cajoled.

Once you made the decision to pad your pants, you urged your parents to drop you off two houses away from school, citing Ládùn as the perfect excuse. "Ládùn is a senior student. If all her boarding school friends keep seeing her parents every day, they'll call her a baby. In fact, let me go with Bòbòólá. Her driver can drop me off."

"Fine, we will drop you in front of the Seventh-day Adventist church, and you can walk to school from there," your father said.

Màámi wasn't convinced, but your father prevailed on her with a kiss. "You can't kiss your way out of everything, Titó," she said.

You thought about what excuse you could give if you were caught stuffing a singlet into your pants. You pictured the judgemental looks that would be plastered on their faces. It was a small price to pay for the reward of giving your buttocks some shape. You had one rule in school: never get too close to any of your mates, so they wouldn't shift the shape of your bumbum. Your chest was filling out, but Màámi didn't think you had outgrown your bralettes. *Maybe I can borrow a real bra from Abigail*, you thought as you looked in the mirror one morning.

Abigail, like you, attended Sunshine College, but she was on a scholarship to your school from her church. Even though you were the same age, she already had a slightly protruding backside and big breasts. One day during interhouse sports practice, you'd seen that she also had hair under her armpits, like your father.

Abigail's mother sold onions at Sábó market, but her competitors spread rumours that she was also a lady of the night alongside the women in Eléyelé—a popular street in Ilé-Ifẹ̀. Ifẹ̀ was a small town, and the people enjoyed gossip. It was the only other excitement they enjoyed apart from the influx of big organisations and churches, and the establishment of international schools that attracted foreigners and rich locals. The women of Eléyelé were workers during the day, but at night, with as little as three hundred naira, a man could find succour between their thighs. These women fucked other women's men and men who were too cowardly to talk to women during the day. There was a time when many of the women were dying, and it was rumoured that a white man had come into town and infected them with HIV. Science had not found a way to curb the spread of the infection at the time. Native doctors and religious leaders scrambled around looking for a cure, but nothing was able to save the women. Eléleyé became a graveyard that most people avoided, even if it meant taking longer routes to their destinations.

"Abigail, please give me any extra bra you have. My mum won't let me wear one," you said at school the following day.

"Hmm . . . okay. No problem, give me until tomorrow. This one I am wearing will be dry after I wash it tomorrow. I have only two. So you can have one."

"I don't understand." Your forehead creased into a frown.

Abigail hissed, "What is confusing about what I just said? I wear my underwear twice before I wash it."

"Abigail! Even your pants?"

"Témì, I can't waste detergent *now*. One bowl of Omò is now three hundred naira. I will wear the pants and bras inside out the next day, not the same way."

"So because of that, you wear pants twice before washing, abi? That's just gross. Is that why you always smell of onions?"

"Témì, your head is not correct! You know my mother sells onions. What am I supposed to smell of when onions take up more space than people in our tiny flat? Miss Clean, abuse me, you hear? With all these boys toasting me, you are the only one complaining about my hygiene. That is your headache."

Borrowing Abigail's bra was out of the question. So you were stuck with just singlets in your pants. You never forgot to take out the singlets before your mother showed up in her Beetle to pick you up. Luckily, she was always fifteen minutes late due to her afternoon meetings that often overran. She worked in the university as an administrative officer. So you had time to take the singlets out and wait around the church, away from the school, so your classmates didn't wonder how you became flat again. You were tired of their teasing.

"She is flat like a board and has long hair touching her back; guess who she is?"

"Témì Lepa Shandy!"

Yes, you laughed with them, because if you cried, you would be labelled as the one who couldn't take a joke. The whole Lepa

Shandy debacle was the reason you dropped out of the debate club that Abigail had encouraged you to join. "You have a sharp mouth, Témì; you might as well use it to win competitions."

You won a few with the team before the boys from the opposing school decided to ruin the experience by heckling you during the postdebate meet and greet.

"Even Lepa dey speak English."

"See-through sisí dey wear oversized coat."

"Winner winner, that wind can blow away."

They heckled a lot of the other girls too, but still, it made you decide to drop out of the team. Whenever you felt a hankering for extracurricular activities, you hid in the library and read a book or knit a sweater.

At the end of the school day, when you left to meet your mother by the church, strange men jeered at you.

"Òpélèngé, come marry me. I go give you baby, and make you fat."

"Ìdí é dà? You no hear me? I say where your yansh?"

On the days your mother sent you to the market, the harassment was twofold. "Màámi, please, do I have to go? Why do you always forget to buy pepper? That aunty with the big head brings it to your office every Thursday. I have a lot of assignments."

"Témì, you were watching a cartoon before I called you. Is it Chika you are calling big head? After she bought you plantain chips last week? Aunty Témì, my oga, is it me that will go? I should let the rice burn, abi? Please just run along and come back quickly. Don't talk to strangers. Thank you, my favourite daughter. Don't tell Ládùn I said that to you." She would wink at you, and tickle

you until you agreed to go. Once you realised you couldn't escape
the chore, you would run from your house until you got to Ìyá
Malik's shop. She knew the usual portions your mother bought:
five hundred naira worth of ata rodo, two hundred naira of toma-
toes, and one hundred naira of onions.

"Témì, how are you, my dear?" Ìyá Malik asked.

"Fine, ma." You'd sit down to rest so you could prepare for the
race back home.

"Ahn ahn, why are you sweating like this? Is someone chasing
you? Do you want *pure water*?"

"No, I am fine, ma. Thank you, ma."

"How is Ládùn? My son will still marry that sister of yours!
Tell your mother I will start selling international spices so that I
can afford Ládùn's bride price."

Ìyá Malik's son was a known street fighter. He'd fought everything and everyone. The market was rowdy, so when you quietly
said, "God forbid," she didn't hear you.

Once you had paid, you would run back home. As you
sprinted, the wind would blow their mockery into your ears.
"Penkeleméèsì . . . sisí . . . can't you hear me calling you?"

It was on market runs that you missed Ládùn the most. If your
sister had been with you, she would have mocked them back.
"See your k-leg, you look like a bush baby. Your mother." She
would stick out her tongue and shoot out her open palm at them.
Sometimes they'd chase you. Other times they were too shocked
to respond, because children in Ilé-Ifẹ̀ were taught never to look
anyone older in the eye, regardless of the situation.

One day, while walking down to a nearby stall to buy bàbá

dúdú and waiting for your mother to be done with Ìyá Malik, a man on a motorbike slowed down beside you and smacked you on the butt. You froze. "Nothing dey there," he hissed.

You ran back and hid behind your mother.

"Ahn ahn, Témì, you are back so quick. Where is your bàbá dúdú?"

You muttered an excuse. As you drove back home, you realised that the singlets were just a temporary fix. Something had to be done, so you came up with a plan to get fat and grow your butt. You started eating late at night because Abigail said her father got fat by doing that.

"Na the fat kill the man. When his people came to drive us from the house, that Aunty Philo wey my mama borrow ten thousand naira raise hand, slap my mama." Abigail only spoke pidgin when riled up.

You needed her to focus. "Abigail, don't worry, you will be a big madam and show them pepper. For now, tell me what kind of food your daddy ate."

"Everything, Témì. Bushmeat, pig, guinea fowl, fùfú with èfó rírò. He ate them all at any time of the day and always asked for seconds. He always said it was only food that could take him away. He was right. It was the food that killed him eventually."

You were not planning to die like her father; you would stop when you started seeing results. You ate your share and then everyone's leftovers. "Please, whatever you don't finish, leave for me."

"Témì, you know I can cook more; why are you so interested in leftovers?" Aunty Jummai would ask. The first time she caught you eating in the kitchen at one a.m., she was aghast. "Why are you eating this late?"

The problem was, despite your increased consumption that was almost becoming gluttonous, all you had to show for it was a big belly. After eating some nights, you would pray to whatever being was up in the skies, but it never answered. You also started to exercise. You got this tip from your mother's exercise tape that she had converted to DVD. A woman named Jane Fonda showed women how to get the perfect tush.

"Ladies, we are now going to work on our behinds. Just bend, now bend; that's it. Do the squat," she instructed. So after school, once you had finished your homework, you did squats in the corridor.

"Témì, what is this one again?" your father asked one evening. He was seated at the dining table opposite the living room, getting ready to grade his students' papers. He usually watched TV to catch up on the news.

"It is a physical education assignment, Daddy. Our teacher says we should do these exercises for thirty days."

"Hmm. Just take it easy."

After a few days, you couldn't keep up with the squats because your muscles started to ache, and the bumbum still hadn't come to light.

You moved on to your next plan. You started drinking Maltina and milk because Bòbóólá shared the details of the concoction her aunt drank after an illness turned her into a skeleton. You and Bòbóólá had been neighbours for as long as you could remember. You grew up together, but your mothers seemed to only tolerate each other. Even though Bọ̀bọọ́lá's parents were lecturers, they lived like politicians. Their family was known for showing off their wealth. At parties, they had talking drummers sing their praises, and they always drove the latest cars with customised plate numbers. Bọ̀bọọ́lá's father often fell out with his colleagues because he was not a union member. Bọ̀bọọ́lá attended the school on campus for the lecturers' children, while you and Abigail were in Sunshine College, outside the campus premises.

You drank so much of the mixture that you fell sick. That was when you stopped taking weight-gain advice from Bọ̀bọọ́lá. Dr. Anyadike came to your bedside one afternoon at the hospital.

"Doctor, I can't be sick," you pleaded in between snorts.

"Well, if you want to get better, you must stop drinking Maltina and milk."

"But I don't want to look like a skeleton." That was what Chetachi, one of your classmates, had called you the last time you were ill.

"Témì, you won't look like a skeleton. Can't you see how your mummy looks? You will eventually look like her." He was a doctor, and doctors never lie. You spent three days in the hospital. You lost all the weight—even on your chest—and you were back to size zero.

You and Ládùn attended the same secondary school and university. She was always four years ahead of you. On your first day of secondary school, Màámi kept crying.

"Màámi, I am coming home this afternoon. Why are you crying like I am going away forever?"

"Témì, you are my last child. The house will be empty."

"No, Aunty Jummai will be at home."

She hissed at you.

"Please, let Daddy drop me off and pick me up today. I don't want to look like a baby to my mates. Let me go in and come out by myself."

"You are always one step ahead, planning everything. You are a reincarnation of my mother," she said as she adjusted your oversized pinafore.

"I know, Màámi; so please listen to your mother and stay at home!"

She laughed and hugged you. "Tell your sister to call your father; he has bought her some stationery. Tell her I will send food to her and Àdùnní next week."

"Okay, ma."

She planted kisses all over your face and gave you extra money for lunch. You planned to give some of it to Ládùn. She needed the money more since she had to stay in the hostel to prepare for her exams. A tall figure approached as you walked through the school gates. "You! Stop there! Where are you going?" You struggled to lift the big sandals that your mother had promised you would grow into. You tripped, falling on your face. Luckily you broke the fall with your palms, but in the process bruised your right palm, causing the skin to peel; the dust from the gravel stained your white pinafore. This was exactly what you had been dreading, and you wished the floor would open up.

"Didn't you hear me?" the voice said again.

"I am going to my class!"

Ládùn had told you about bullying and how to deal with it in preparation for your first day. She said you should never look a bully in the eye. "Bullies are like small gods that are hungry. If you square up to them, they will pounce. Look down and just keep saying, 'My sister is Omoládùn Tóyèbí.'"

"Why?"

"Because your mouth is sharp, Témì, and if you run it before I can rescue you, they will beat you black and blue."

"Okay o. I will look down and say your name. I will chant it like a sermon. Hello, Ládùn Tóyèbí is my sister. Hello, don't worry about my name; Ládùn Tóyèbí is my sister." You started to sing, dancing in circles around her. A few chants later, Ládùn grabbed you as you kept teasing her.

"Round one!" She tackled you and threw you on the bed.

It was a good thing you listened when Ládùn advised you, because this tall figure sounded and looked like a bully.

The girl's tight skirt, which was stifling the life out of her skinny thighs, told you she had to be a prefect. "What is your name?"

"My sister is Omoládùn Tóyèbí." You didn't look up even though your palms hurt.

"You are Ládùn's sister?" Her voice changed, and she shot her hand out to help you up. "You don't look alike."

You had heard this all your life. Where you were skinny, Ládùn was slender; where you were flat-chested, Ládùn had oranges; and while there was an obvious absence of a butt for you, Ládùn had started shaping out nicely. But that wasn't all she meant—you already had a stain on your clothes on your first day, and you could bet Ládùn never had stains.

"She has been talking nonstop about you. Let me take you to the washroom."

"Thank you."

She walked through the car park toward a block of classrooms, and you hurried to keep up with her long strides. Across the block of classrooms was a football pitch complete with goalposts on both ends. The fences bordering that side of the compound were tall enough to prove a challenge to boarding students who hoped to break school rules and explore outside those walls, but short enough that the palm trees that grew from the next compound overshadowed them. A dusty purple-and-white school bus was parked beside the entrance of the block. You counted the stairs as you climbed to the first floor. You dreaded the daily exercise because it meant you would lose some flesh. She led you down a corridor, flanked on both sides by classroom doors. The noise the students made unnerved you. You wondered how they were able to get any learning done. No wonder Ládùn craved silence whenever she came home.

"Here is your classroom. You will return here after washing your pinafore," the girl said, pointing at a nondescript door on the left.

The senior moved on to the end of the corridor. The smell of bleach stung your nostrils as you approached. "This is the toilet," she said, handing you a sachet of detergent from her fanny pack. "Wash up quickly and head to class. I'll let your sister know where to find you."

"Thank you."

You tried to wash the stain off, but you ended up making it worse, leaving a map-shaped patch on your pinafore. Thankfully Ládùn heard of your arrival and came to your class with a thick sweater.

The boys made secondary school a nightmare. They made fun of the girls who they believed weren't pretty or those whose busts were not as big as they would have liked. They made lists of girls they fancied spending their Valentine's Day with, but your name was never included. They drew caricatures of female students on the blackboard, and when it was your turn, they drew a stick figure with lots of hair, and made scornful jokes.

"Témì aka small bumbum!"

"Lepa Shandy."

"Jesus will resurrect the yansh one day!"

Aside from making jokes, they also organised awards every year. They called it the April Fool's Awards. You won Miss Curvy two years in a row. Désólá, a student with sickle cell anaemia, was awarded Most Athletic. She was slender like you. Her yellow eyes were kind, and she always had chocolates to spare.

"I can't cope with these nasty boys who won't stop teasing me. The silence from the teachers makes matters worse. Is it my fault that I am SS? I am going back to England! I'll learn about Nigeria through books," she said in distress. Her British accent got thicker whenever she was emotional. When Désólá waved goodbye to you and Abigail, a part of you was jealous.

✳

By the time you got to your third year of junior secondary school, Ládùn had graduated. In a surprising turn of events, a new student joined your class, having secured a transfer from Lagos. There were rumours that he was able to gain admission into JSS3 only because his aunt had close contact with the principal. His name was Ikenna, or IK for short. He was the subject of gossip for weeks after.

"I hear his parents do not live in Nigeria."

"Not true! Look at how you are spreading rumours. They are from Abia state, but are very poor, I hear."

"How do all these people know about our school?"

"You think it is easy to win the Cowbell Mathematics Competition three years in a row?"

"Oh . . ."

"He has a brother who is in boarding school. I heard that the parents gave him to the rich aunt who wanted to help them."

"He is so cute!"

IK was different from his peers. He was neither interested in the most beautiful girls in the class nor the popular ones. He liked politics, and started conversations that he was convinced would change the world. You became friends with him a week after he arrived. He was lanky, was the colour of caramel, and was by far the tallest in your class. You found comfort in talking to another Lepa Shandy.

"Hi, my name is Témì," you said one day as he was about to go get lunch.

"I know you. You scored the highest in business studies."

You smiled because he was impressed by your brains, as opposed to your looks. "*You* came second."

"I plan to beat you next time."

That was how you and IK became close. You found out that his parents lived in Abia because his mother got a job as the head of the sociology department at Abia State University. His father was an auto-parts dealer.

"He is a businessman. Anywhere money can be made, you will find my father there. My brother is in boarding school in Ògùn state. I guess my parents love the Yoruba people," IK said one afternoon. When people made jokes about your frame, he confronted them and made them apologise. You wanted him to feel your gratitude, so you always packed lunch for him and brought him anything you thought he needed.

"Témì, please don't pack all my food for IK."

"Yes, Màámi."

Soon you introduced him to Bòbòólá and Abigail. Màámi had no choice but to accept him. Ládùn liked him.

"This IK of yours, are you sure he is not your boyfriend?"

"Ládùn, he is one of my best friends, just like you, Bòbòólá, and Abigail."

"Okay, so will you give me your food for the week like you give IK?"

"Stop now—"

"I am teasing you. I like your friends. I think you and IK would make a cute couple at the right time. Right now, don't even think about it."

"He is just my friend o."

"Yeah, right."

IK and Abigail made everything better.

A year later, in your first term of senior secondary school, a boy called Evidence was introduced to your class. He was the only one whose looks trumped IK's in your eyes. He was six feet tall; his long lashes and beautiful dimples were the envy of many girls.

"I heard he has a girlfriend, and she is a big girl," one of your classmates typed in the WhatsApp group that the girls created for circulating and discussing assignments. They probably added you to the group because you were the most brilliant of them all. Apart from the first day, no one discussed homework—only boys and heartbreaks.

"This is the first time in my life that I find the name Evidence sexy. I want him to do whatever he likes to me," the daughter of a popular politician in Ilé-Ifẹ̀ typed.

"Like . . . do you see his lips? Sooo pink."

"You people should go and sleep. I pray the matron catches you with all those phones you are hiding in the hostel," Abigail responded, and the group went silent. Abigail had gained their respect the day she beat up the class bully without getting as much as a scratch.

You also fantasised about Evidence, but you were never going to admit it out loud. So when Evidence started talking to you often and even holding your hand in public, you felt the flatness of your buttocks didn't bother him. A week before the annual dance that the school held for senior secondary students, boys typically asked the girls they admired out, and you had always found yourself with IK, since no one ever asked you. Although he never complained, you knew he had his eye on Tòkunbò, the most beautiful girl in the year below. Tòkunbò's dark skin was so shiny and smooth that it looked like it was painted by the most skillful hands. Her near-perfect dentition was constantly on display whenever she threw back her neck in laughter, grazing his arms slightly. IK's jokes were not that funny.

When Evidence asked you to be his partner, you felt immense relief.

IK didn't seem too sure. "Ahn ahn, Témì, you know it is always you and me *now*. Why would you say yes to Evidence?"

"IK, ask Tòkunbò to the dance. I know you like her. You don't have to babysit me." The guilty look on his face told you that you were right about his feelings for Tòkunbò.

On the day of the dance, Ládùn packed your hair into a cute doughnut. You put an extra singlet in your bag, to stuff later into your jean skirt, paired this with a ruffled top, applied some powder, and used a little bit of lip gloss.

"Témì, you look so beautiful." Ládùn stepped back to admire you.

"Thank you, Ládùn."

You sprayed your mother's perfume, and even your parents complimented your looks. If Evidence asked you to be his girlfriend, you would definitely say yes.

"Témì, I can't wait to see how beautiful you will be when you grow up," Evidence said shyly.

You held your breath in anticipation as you bopped to Wizkid's "Love My Baby."

He continued, "I swear, your future boyfriend is going to be so lucky. Meanwhile, is Abigail single, please?" That was the last time you let yourself fall for the opposite gender.

You stopped wearing underwear when you turned fifteen. You became a staunch believer in your small bumbum shaking furiously to compensate for its lack of fat. You were now used to your ass starting conversations. If people were going to stare, you would at least keep their eyes busy. Most days, you played songs in your head to accompany the reckless jiggle—Reekado Banks's "Problem," and sometimes Sean Paul's "Shake That Thing" also ended up in the mix. Your wide-ranging taste in music helped you achieve your small-yansh-shaking goal every day.

"Wa, Témì, please, what is the purpose of this pantlessness? Why are you stressing everyone with yansh? The way your butt cheeks are dancing will only attract useless men." Aunty Jummai's eyes followed you around the house.

"I am wearing underwear, Aunty."

"No, you are not. I have never seen your underwear on the washing line in the backyard. Do you wash your pata and keep it in your bag? Who will marry you? My dear, if I can notice the buttocks, imagine the erotic images you will evoke in the minds of outsiders. Your father is a respected professor. Please, represent this family well."

Other people were rude like she was too. They spoke to you with their eyes—they looked at your ass and then directly at you, as if to say, *How dare you come out of your house with your inverted buttocks jiggling?*

In your final term, during a Monday morning assembly, Cheta-chi, the class prankster, stuck a note on the back of your blouse. It read, "My big butt brings all the boys to the yard." That week, you were all alone. IK was away from school for a debate, and Abigail was attending a family engagement in the east. Her father's family had been back in touch to offer her mother a portion of her late husband's estate, if she agreed to move back to Awka so Abigail could be raised under the watchful eye of her father's family.

When you finished leading the prayers, you turned to join the other students. To your shock, the principal called your full name.

"Témì Tóyèbí, please take that note off."

"What note, sir?"

"The one on your back, young lady."

Laughter erupted as you rushed back to join your class line. You heard snide comments from students as they trooped out of the hall after the assembly.

"Mopstick Témì."

"How is it that someone has stayed flat for six years?"

"Her sister is a perfect figure eight."

The embarrassment stayed with you even after graduation.

To make the week even worse, the class yearbook came out. Whereas Abigail was almost everyone's crush, *you* were on the good friend/sister list.

Ládùn was admitted to Obáfémi Awólówò University, even though her preference was to attend university in Jos. Your father flatly refused. "My first fruit, you know I never say no to you. But this is a no. You are attending OAU." He was worried about the intertribal unrest in Plateau state. That sealed the matter and made it easy for your parents to nudge you toward attending the same university.

Abigail and her mother had moved east after secondary school, so you could only keep in touch via Facebook and BlackBerry Messenger. It was just you, IK, and sometimes Bòbóọlá who would hang out on weekends. You were the three musketeers.

In Ládùn's final year, you were admitted to the Department of English and Literary Studies, while Bòbóọlá and IK were offered places in the Department of International Relations. You were overjoyed to maintain some of the friendships that you had culti- vated in your childhood. It was later that you overheard your mother saying that Bòbóọlá's place had been bought. You didn't care how Bòbóọlá got in; you were just happy she did.

You knew Bòbóọlá had a difficult relationship with her par- ents. Shortly after the admission lists were made public, Bòbóọlá stopped by, clearly downcast. "My mother always came first in school; my father won all the academic awards when he was in university. How am I supposed to live up to their expectations?"

"I think they just want you to do better." You couldn't think of anything else to say.

"Témì, not everybody is like you. I may be smart in other ways, but since they are lecturers, the only thing that matters to them is academic excellence. I am their only child. I am an utter disgrace to them for not being an academic star," Bòbọọlá lamented.

"I think 'disgrace' is a bit harsh."

Bòbọọlá did things out of character. During her first year of senior secondary school, she was caught kissing a boy in the back of the school library by one of the cleaners, who promptly reported her to the principal. She only escaped suspension because her father promised the principal a trip to Ghana.

"Témì, I can't believe that man let me go because he wanted to visit Ghana," Bòbọọlá narrated months after.

Most of her actions were attention-seeking. It always worked because it resulted in her parents calling on you to help them out.

"Please speak to Bòbọọlá. Why can't she just be normal?"

"I will talk to her, ma."

Abigail stopped reaching out to you as soon as you got into OAU. She was going to study medicine in the United States of America—at least that's what she wrote in her last message. Maybe she got weighed down with classes, because she went from chatting with you every day to occasionally liking your posts on social media.

You were going to send her a message to ask what had happened, but assignments and tests got in the way. You decided IK and Bòbọọlá were all you needed. Even though Ládùn was available and you sometimes crashed in her hostel, she had her own group of friends.

"One day, you and Ikenna will end up together," Bòbóọlá teased.

"You people should stop. He is my best friend, just as you are."

"Your best friend who is now very handsome."

"He doesn't look any different from when we were in secondary school." You were lying, and she knew it.

IK and Bòbóọlá were like cat and mouse. Even when you convened in the lecture halls to revise overnight, they didn't stop going at each other's throats.

"Ikenna, take it easy with the girls; HIV is real *o*," Bòbóọlá would say to him whenever she was spoiling for a fight.

"Says the girl who is dating a notorious cultist," IK would retort.

"Please, you people can fight later," you would say. "For now, let's read. This is just our first year. You should both wait until we get to year three before becoming ashéwós." That always kept them quiet.

The first year was spent with the three of you trying to keep up with the chaotic schedule of lectures and navigating the distances between most lecture halls. Once classes were over, you, Bòbóọlá, and IK gathered at New Buka to eat before you went back to quarters or Ládùn's hostel. IK's hostel was Awolowo Hall, and Bòbóọlá lived wherever her boo of the moment resided. That was your routine.

Everything was going great until the night of Ládùn's graduation.

LÁDÙN'S BODY

I always had a love-hate relationship with my body. Yes, I loved that it was healthy, but I hated that it developed too early, making me the centre of unwanted attention. I couldn't quite understand why it had such an effect on men. It drew them to me like alates to a fluorescent bulb. They all wanted to touch me; sometimes doing so without my consent. What exactly was wrong with me that made men stare endlessly? Why couldn't I be straight as a pencil, narrow and athletic?

"Please stop touching me!" I wanted to scream, but it was not only strangers who touched me. It was also family friends, schoolmates, familiar faces, so it was hard to tell them to fuck off. Who told men that putting their slobbering tongues in my ear was appealing?

The first time someone invaded my personal space was at a family friend's house. *Why is this boy licking my face?* was my first thought as I sat in Dr. Anyadike's dark grey living room, distracting myself with the portraits of former presidents hanging on the wall.

In the early hours, Témì had been rushed to the hospital. Her tummy was hard as stone, and her groaning interrupted my slumber. "Ládùn, go and call Màámi, please."

My mother was panting when she entered our bedroom. "Why are you always drinking malt and milk?"

"Màámi, please, I want to poo-poo!" Témì rocked back and forth, hugging her slim frame.

At dawn, Dr. Anyadike asked my mother to bring Témì to the clinic.

"Mum, why can't I come with you?"

"Témì is ill; your sister needs all my attention."

"This is why I wanted to go with Daddy." My father was at a conference in Lókója, presenting a paper.

"Ládùn, just stay with Mummy Udoka. I will be back." She turned to Udoka's mother. "Please don't let her out of your sight," she said.

"Don't worry. I will be here with her," Mrs. Anyadike assured my mum.

As soon as my mother drove off, Mrs. Anyadike disappeared upstairs. A few minutes later, her tree of a son, Udoka, came out of nowhere. He sat close to me on the two-seater; his fingers drummed near my left thigh. When I turned to face him, he forced his lips on mine and shoved his tongue through my teeth.

I pushed as hard as I could. "Udoka, what are you doing?"

"Ládùn, you are so beautiful. I can't wait for you to grow up so we can marry."

"So you know I am not grown up yet, and still you are kissing me. I am only fourteen!"

"So? I am just two years older! You know what? I will tell my mum this evening to come and see your parents so that as soon as you turn eighteen, we can get married!" Udoka said, running his hand up my thigh. He stopped midway and looked at me with a smile that made my tummy turn.

Why did his mother leave me alone with him? What am I going to do?

My mother had always warned me, "Ládùn, don't ever be alone with a man."

Suddenly, he said, "You know what? Let me not touch you now. I will wait until we are married."

The clown was serious. "Okay, Udoka. When our parents return, talk to them."

My mother returned almost immediately, so he didn't get the chance. Témì had been admitted to the hospital.

Three days later, Témì was back home, and her neck seemed to have grown longer, with her collarbones protruding. She spent many nights crying on her bed. I was awake those nights thinking about how to tell my parents about Udoka.

"Témì, what is wrong? Did something happen at the hospital? Why did you drink so much milk and malt?" I asked her after the fourth night of hearing her sniffles.

"I am tired of being Ọ̀pẹ́lẹ́ngẹ́. I want to be fat."

"But Témì, you and I are the same."

"No, we are not!" She cried harder. "Ládùn, I don't want to go back to school this skinny."

"Skinny ke?"

"Yes! I was already thin. Now after this hospital admission, I look like a skeleton!" she responded, tears running down her face.

I helped her up and led her to the mirror that separated both our beds. "Can you see how beautiful you are?" I asked, wiping her tears with my nightie sleeve.

"Me, beautiful?" She looked up at me with hopeful eyes.

"Very beautiful. You are the most beautiful girl in the world, and when you grow up, you are going to be Miss World." She still looked sad, so I tickled her under her chin until she started to laugh. We snuck out to the living room and watched reruns of her favourite television programme, *Tales by Moonlight*. We soon forgot our worries and sang along to the theme song. I didn't tell my parents about Udoka. I blamed his actions on temporary insanity.

Mr. Ogonna, the physics teacher, was the next man to touch me. He was new to our school and very popular with the girls, especially my best friend, Àdùnní. Àdùnní was half Yoruba, from her father's side, and half American. For someone who had lived in the United States up until three years before, she spoke better Yoruba than some of us who were indigenes of Ilé-Ifẹ̀. To understand her, I always had to stare intently at her lips. Her parents were divorced. While Àdùnní's mother stayed behind in the United States, her father now lived in Ìjẹ̀bú Òde. He'd sent Àdùnní to live with his sister in Ilé-Ifẹ̀, who promptly shipped her off to boarding school. "Have you guys seen the new teacher? He is drop-dead gorgeous!" Àdùnní gushed, plopping down onto the seat we shared during the long break one Friday. A small crowd quickly gathered around us. She always had the best gist, and we knew we were in for a treat.

"Ládùn, have *you* seen the teacher?" Jídé asked me. I knew he was only trying to get my attention.

"No, I have not."

Jídé leaned on my desk. I could smell the black currant on his breath. "Ládùn, Ládùn, one day, one day, you will be mine," he whispered in my right ear, and swaggered back to his seat. Jídé was not bad-looking; he just had a loose mouth and made sure to brag about every girl in class he had kissed. "Mr. Ogonna's shoulders are so broad and strong," Lateefa said, adjusting her hijab.

"Lateefa! How do you know what his shoulders feel like?" Àdùnní asked.

Lateefa ignored the question and kept mooning over Mr. Ogonna, going into a level of detail that left me wondering how she knew so much about him. I wanted to remind her that she was already betrothed to the imam at the mosque opposite our school. We knew the imam had enrolled her in Sunshine College to keep an eye on her. Lateefa, nonetheless, acted like he didn't exist. We were in SS2, but she was already on her sixth boyfriend, and there were rumours that she had done things with all of them.

"As long as she is not having sex, she will be fine. The imam will meet her untouched," Àdùnní told me one evening after sharing stories of Lateefa's latest conquests.

"I really hope she doesn't marry that imam. He's too old for her."

"Ládùn, the man is rich, and he's building her a house. She will marry him."

Three days later, the famous Mr. Ogonna was in my class. All the girls stared at him dreamily with wide smiles plastered on their faces. Some of them had their hair redone; some had used mascara, so they batted their lashes at him when he introduced him-self. Even the guys were mesmerised. The class, which was usually noisier than Sábó market, was dead silent. I watched the entire scene unfold, amused. I was not one of the girls fawning over him. I didn't even talk to him outside class, so I was shocked when, a month later, he palmed my breasts and tried to kiss me. That afternoon, I had gone to submit the class assignment. I had stepped in as the assistant class captain since the captain was in-disposed. Mr. Ogonna had instructed me to bring the practical manuals to him at the end of the school day. He came round, pretending to examine the graphs, then pinned me against the desk. I felt something hard poking my belly while he sought my mouth with his. I pushed him off with all my strength, and he reeled back, his eyes blazing.

"Ládùn, I want you!"

"I am fourteen, sir."

"And I am thirty-four."

"Does this seem okay to you, sir? Please don't do that again. I respect you."

"I want to marry you, Ládùn. You are not like the other wild girls. I want you to be my wife."

Here we go again. Another man telling me he wants to marry me. His words swarmed like bees around my ears. Was there something about me that told men that I was looking for a hus-band when I didn't even know what my plan for the next day was? "Please, sir, find someone your own age. I will not be avail-able to deliver manuals from tomorrow. I will ask Jídé to bring you anything else you need." I ran toward his door and heaved a sigh of relief when it gave way. *These teachers! If the math teacher wasn't trying to kill you with his body odour, the physics teacher was trying to grope you.* That was the last time I went to any male teacher's office. I wished every teacher was like my father, who only had eyes for my mother. That term, I got a C in physics. The whole family was gathered in our living room. Our parents sat, sifting through our report cards, while Témì and I stood before them. "Ládùn, why are your physics results so bad?" my mother queried.

"I don't know, ma."

"What do you mean you don't know?" She inched forward and sat on the very edge of her seat.

My father came to my aid. "Baby, Ládùn is a brilliant girl; she scored high marks in other subjects."

"Tító! Why are you always shielding this girl from taking responsibility for her actions?"

"I am sorry." My father looked genuinely contrite. "Ládùn, answer your mother, please."

My father's words washed over her like cold water. "It's okay. Ládùn, if you are having issues with a particular subject, just tell us. We will help you."

"Okay, ma."

My mother shifted her attention to Témì. "Madam Témì, good results all around. But don't think I did not see the fountain pen you brought home yesterday. I know we didn't buy that type for you. If you don't stop being mischievous, I will flog you one day! Trouble is dancing on your head!"

"Màámi, it belongs to Bòbọ́lá. If you don't believe me, you

can go to their house to check." Témì moved closer to our mother, arms akimbo.

"Témì, do you want to beat me? Why are you standing over me?"

Témì took a step back and stood closer to our father. "Daddy, can you hear what Màámi is saying? Why would I want to beat her?"

My father smiled at Témì. "Your mouth will get you into trouble with your mother someday. So the presents, as promised. Ládùn came fourth, and Témì—"

"Témì was first, so you have to buy her that bicycle; Ládùn gets nothing," Mummy cut in quickly. My dad smiled in agreement.

"Ah, thank you, Màámi. Thank you, Daddy. I promise that my grades won't fall."

"Well done, girls! Go to your room," my mother said.

I did not mention the incident with Mr. Ogonna, but I decided to start wearing oversized clothes. Perhaps my body was the reason men acted inappropriately around me.

"Ládùn, please, what are you wearing? What is this?" Àdùnní asked me on the first day of the next term. I looked down at my frumpy skirt. It was not as fashionable as the one I usually wore.

"My other uniform is torn. I will fix it soon," I lied.

"Why didn't you slim-fit this one in the meantime? Now you look like Mrs. Pepper, the matron."

"Thank you very much, Agbani Darego. Please, if you don't want to be seen with me, keep your distance."

"Ahn ahn, Ládùn. It is not that serious. Even with this baggy thing, you are still the most beautiful girl in the class," she replied. That was one thing I liked about Àdùnní. She was never envious.

Although Mr. Ogonna invited me to his office a couple more times, I always found a way to dodge him. He finally resigned in disgrace a year later after impregnating Lateefa. Her family forced him to marry her. Pictures of their Nikah circulated the school. In them, he looked like he had been sentenced to jail, with an angry expression on his face, as Lateefah beamed from ear to ear, grateful she didn't end up with the imam. The school tried to cover up the incident so that our parents wouldn't find out. Sunshine College was a regular winner of mathematics competitions in Nigeria. The scandal set classrooms abuzz with many versions of what happened. "I can't believe that man slept with Lateefa."

"Did you not see her voluptuous front and backyard? Even me sef don toast am!"

All my classmates had opinions. The girls seemed really upset, while Àdùnní was quiet and withdrawn.

"Àdùnní, are you okay?"

"I am just tired of these useless men."

Later on, I found her crying in the hostel. All students were required to live in the hostel during their final year of senior secondary school, although it had been home to Àdùnní and me since SS2. I was not going to be without my soul sister, and my parents understood this.

"I slept with him, Ládùn. I let that man fuck me."

My heart dropped as I sat beside her on the lower bunk. I whispered, "Are you okay? Are you—"

"I am too smart to get pregnant. Me and Lateefa were sharing community penis. I am just angry. He said he loved me!"

I draped an arm around her shoulders as she relayed what had transpired between her and Mr. Ogonna.

"Let's not date anyone until we are done with secondary school," I suggested.

"I hear you. The truth is, I was just bored. And he just seemed so nice. My parents have forgotten me here. My aunt couldn't care less; I am her cash cow. Even when I go home during the holidays, she doesn't have time for me."

"You know you can always come to my house. My parents love you. Témì and I are your sisters."

"Thank you."

School rules became more stringent after Mr. Ogonna left. Mrs. Pepper punished a student for standing too close to her dance partner. The poor girl cut grass for a week. After that, the students found ingenious ways to escape punishment. Whenever a dance party was organised for us, I got permission to go home to avoid any of the drama going on in school—I much preferred hanging out with Témì anyway. We went around plucking guava from low branches and buying ice cream. Never mind that we spent the next day on the toilet, wriggling in discomfort as we emptied our bowels.

During the holidays, there were rumours about wild parties, where some of the students engaged in intercourse. My experiences with men made it easier for me to avoid such parties.

"I would have invited you to Jídé's party, but I know your parents are like hawks. They watch you people."

I didn't bother to correct Àdùnní, but she must have seen the concerned look on my face.

"Don't worry, Ládùn. I am not doing anything with those boys."

In my final year, I became the social prefect, which gave me the perfect opportunity to watch over Témì in my free time. I didn't want any male teachers preying on her. I wanted her to be trauma-free, as she was already growing into a very attractive girl. On one of the weekends I was home, my father and I were lounging in the living room when he asked, "My first fruit, please, why are you always wearing oversized clothes?"

A lump formed in my throat. "Daddy, if I tell you, promise me you won't tell Mum." I told him about the many times men had tried to grope me and about Mr. Ogonna.

"What? That son of a—" He stood immediately and paced around the coffee table, his hands clenching and unclenching.

"Daddy, are you angry with me?"

"My first fruit, I am angry, but not with you. Some men can be shameless." He walked back to his favourite chair and motioned me closer. "I have to tell your mother. She needs to know, especially since Témì is still in that school. Also, please don't blame yourself. This isn't your fault."

That evening, my mother was inconsolable. She invited the principal to dinner the next day and waited for him to start eating before she spoke. "My child performed poorly in physics because your teacher was trying to have his way with her! Please, in the name of our Lord Jesus, how did a child molester end up teaching in your school?"

"We put him through five interviews, ma," he answered, refusing to meet her gaze.

"Yet you ended up with a pervert? Is it your school's interview process we should blame or you?"

"I am so sorry, ma."

"Témì will not be a boarder in her senior year. I will drop her off every day. You should be thankful that we are not involving the police! Next time, do not employ paedophiles."

"Such an abomination will not repeat itself, ma." The man stammered his way through the rest of the dinner. My mother had made the food extra spicy, and his bald head was covered in sweat as he chewed his pounded yam with ilá alásèpò and goat meat.

I sat with my parents and watched them berate the principal. When he left, my mother cradled me. "Ládùn, you must always tell us if any man makes you uncomfortable. You and your sister are all we have."

"Yes, ma."

Over time, I stopped wearing oversized clothes.

I fell in love while waiting to resume university. We ran into each other at Fajuyi junction. I was waiting for Àdùnní at Major Foods, a popular cafeteria in Ilé-Ifè, when he came in with his mother. He approached me as I absentmindedly nibbled on a spicy fish roll.

"Excuse me, aren't you Ládùn?"

"Yes, I am."

"You probably don't remember me, but I was in SS1 when you were in JSS1. My name is Mofẹ́." He flashed a dimpled smile at me.

I couldn't remember him. "Oh!" His grey monochromatic denim look with matching Skechers encouraged me to continue the conversation. "Hi, Mofẹ́. Long time."

"I can't stay long. I am driving my mum around today. We came from Lagos to Ilé-Ifẹ̀ to sort out some family business. My parents have a house here. Please, can I have your number?"

"Sure!" I punched my number into his phone. He dialled it at once, and I felt the vibration in my pocket.

"I study in the UK now, but I come back to Nigeria every summer."

"Oh!" *Why was this drop-dead gorgeous dude sharing all this information with me?* He turned to walk away, and I noted the way his jeans hugged his lanky frame. His mother, standing by the till, gave me a look of approval.

"Good afternoon, ma." I bowed as low as the table would allow.

"How are you, my dear?" She looked familiar. I later learnt that she was the registrar of the university I was applying to, and her husband supplied fish to most university cafeterias across Nigeria. Mofẹ́ was their only child.

Mofẹ́ called at dusk that day. We reminisced about our years at Sunshine College. He told me that he had always had a crush on me, but he didn't think it was appropriate to approach me, given that he was three years ahead. Soon enough, it became my daily routine to spend my days studying for my University Tertiary Matriculation Exam in my father's office and to hang out with Mofẹ́ in the evening. Sometimes we would go for chicken and chips at Kays Chippy; other times we talked on the phone until our voices grew hoarse and our eyelids closed with fatigue.

The night before he left for the UK, we sat in the campus amphitheatre.

"Ládùn, I am in love with you. Please be mine."

"I am yours."

And that was it! Mofẹ́ was a gentleman. He didn't make me feel uncomfortable and didn't touch me without my permission. That night, I leaned in, just as Àdùnní taught me. He tasted minty, and his beard tickled my chin. My heart beat madly in my chest. It was my first kiss.

Two years into our relationship, our families hadn't met formally, but our mothers greeted each other occasionally.

"How is our baby girl?" his mum would tease over the phone.

"Your son is taking very good care of her," my mother would giggle. Mofẹ́ loved me like my father loved my mother.

We fell deeper in love each passing year. Whenever Mofẹ́ was unable to visit Nigeria, we took advantage of the four hours of free call allowance between midnight and four a.m., talking about everything and nothing. A few times, he had fondled my breasts through my clothes, and when he wanted me to feel how much he desired me, he moved my hand down to stroke him. All of it made me heady with longing, but I always stopped us before we took a step further.

"Mofẹ́, please. I don't think we are ready yet."

"It's fine, I can live with my blue balls for now, my love," he would say, but I could see in his eyes that it was not, and I was worried that UK girls would give him what I wasn't.

It was the end of my second year of university, and we laid in the back seat of his father's Volvo, the dark shadow of Moremi Hall in the distance.

"Babe, I've been meaning to tell you. I am not sure if I can come to Nigeria next summer."

"Oh." I looked out of the window.

"If your parents are open to it, you can come to Nottingham and spend the summer with me."

"Yes! Yes! Yes!" I squealed and did an excited jiggle.

I waited six months to bring the matter up with my parents.

"The answer is no!" my mother said when I asked both of them over Sunday lunch.

"Mummy, please."

"No."

I turned to look at my father, pleading with my eyes. "Daddy, Mofẹ́ and I are waiting until we get married."

"Ehen? Because you and he are not young adults with raging hormones, abi? Lecture us some more, please. I have seen the two of you together." My mother folded her hands across her chest. "We can't afford to take you and Témì to the UK yet. Be satisfied with what your parents give you! Until that boy comes to ask for your hand in marriage, you are going nowhere."

"Ládùn, go to your room," my father said to me after a few seconds of silence. I walked back into the room and waited.

An hour later, my mother burst into the room. "You can go. Your father and I have agreed, on the condition that we speak to Mofẹ́'s parents beforehand."

My eyes welled up. "Thank—"

She walked out.

I couldn't wait to tell Àdùnní. "After the verbal beating from my mother, I am determined to have sex with Mofẹ́ over these holidays, and there's nothing anyone can do to stop me."

"Ahn ahn, where was this Ládùn during our secondary school days?" she asked.

Mofẹ́'s mother let me stay in their house while I applied for my visa. It wasn't as awkward as I thought it would be. I tried to be helpful around the house as my mother advised. Two weeks later, my visa was approved. Mofẹ́'s parents used their connections to fast-track the visa application. His mother handed me a second suitcase to travel with. "Ládùn, please give him this crayfish, garri, and Poundo yam. Tell him I'll bring the rest with me in another two months."

"Okay, ma."

"You people should call your parents once a day so your mother's mind will be at peace."

"Yes, ma."

Once I landed, I called home.

"Ládùn, give the phone to Mofẹ́," Témì instructed me.

I handed the phone to Mofẹ́, who listened for a few seconds and said, "I will send them through your sister."

"Thank you!" I heard her scream. Mofẹ́ handed the phone back to me after speaking with my parents.

"You people should not do anything *o*," my mother said before my father snatched the phone from her and ended the call.

We took the train back to the apartment he shared with a Nigerian roommate, who had gone to stay with his girlfriend to give us some space.

"I don't know why he did that; I told him we are not doing anything. This is just a vacation for me and my baby!" Mofẹ́ said excitedly as he arranged my bags in his closet.

"I am very happy to be here."

"Me too!" His dimples winked at me as he bent to kiss me. "We are going to have so much fun! Change into something nice and let's go out. The UK and Nigeria are in the same time zone. Or are you tired?"

"I want to go everywhere!" I put on a pink blouse, jeans, and the boots he had given me as my welcome gift once we got to his house, then a jacket from Zara. We went to his university campus in Nottingham, and he showed me off to all his friends. I couldn't stop smiling through all their "She is so fine" and "Oi, mate, your babe is peng!" My thoughts were on the night to come. He took me to Nando's, where we shared a chicken burger, and then we finally went back to the flat.

I showered quickly, sprayed some of my mother's Kenzo perfume behind my ears, and laid on the bed after putting on the lingerie I had purchased two days before at GOC Boutique.

"Mofẹ́! What are you doing? What's taking so long?"

"I am coming, love. Trying to finish up something." I heard him shuffling around in the living room.

He came into the bedroom a few minutes later. When he noticed me on the bed, his jaw twitched. "Ládùn, fuck!"

"Like what you see?"

"Fuck!" he repeated. He advanced toward me and then stopped halfway and backpedalled into the bathroom. I heard the shower running. Several minutes later, he reappeared with a pink towel tied around his waist.

"Mofẹ, there is soap behind your ears."

Two minutes later, he was on the bed with me. "You are the most beautiful woman I have ever seen in my life. I love you, Ládùn. I will love you until I die!"

I sat up slowly. "I love you too."

"Are you sure about this, Ládùn? I can wait." His selflessness made me want him more.

"Mofẹ, I see how you look at me. We are going to be married eventually. So why not?"

"Okay." He pulled me closer and then stopped again.

"Mofẹ, it's okay. I want you too." I pressed myself against him, kissing his lips.

"I want to marry you, Ládùn, and I want you to carry our children."

My chest tightened. This man had my heart. "I want to marry you too."

He looked deep into my eyes. "I promise I'll be gentle this time." He claimed my mouth with his.

"Don't scare me, please," I mumbled against his lips.

"I told you, I'll be gentle." He laughed. "Shall we continue?"

"Yes, please."

He pushed me against the pillows while his tongue played with mine. He planted little kisses on my neck and nuzzled his way to my breasts. My legs turned to jelly when he sucked through the mesh. He pinned both hands above my head and blew on my nipple. "Relax, baby," he whispered.

His mouth went to my other nipple while his left hand squeezed the right breast softly. The sensations running through me had me thrashing around on the bed, so he stiffened his body to pin me down. He came back to my lips, and his tongue sunk deeper into my mouth. His knee slid between my legs, and his left hand left my breast and played with my bush. His hot penis pulsated furiously against my belly.

"I am so hard; can you feel me?" he whispered into my left ear, biting my earlobe gently. "Don't be scared." His fingertips massaged my clit. "Ìyàwó mi, let me use my fingers. We will try with my dick another time. I don't want to hurt you." His glassy eyes searched my face.

"No, Mofẹ́. Even if it hurts, let's try." I held his penis in my hand, feeling the moist tip of the cap. I stroked it as Àdùnní had taught me before I travelled.

He pushed my knees toward my chest. His penis sought entrance.

"You are so wet, baby. Fuck!" he said against my lips. "Can you feel how hard I am for you?" He started to enter me gently.

The pain ran straight up my spine. I could feel him slowly tearing through. He saw me wince and mouthed, *Sorry*. "You are so tight, but I can feel your wetness. Please, can I move inside you? I may die if I don't."

"M . . . moove." My vision was blurry with tears.

He started slowly. There was pain, but there was pleasure too. So I closed my eyes and gave myself up to the waves of ecstasy.

Mofẹ́ and I went out during the days and spent our nights learning each other's bodies. He taught me many things. Who knew that my body had so many pleasure points?

On the day I left for Nigeria, I wanted to beg him to stay, but he beat me to it. "Ládùn, how will I cope without you?"

"We have December to look forward to." I hugged him and buried my face in his jacket so it could soak up my tears.

"If you cry, I will cry too, Ládùn."

We sat hand in hand until my flight was called. As I waved goodbye, tears streamed down my face once more.

My final year at university, Mofẹ́ and I began making plans for my relocation to the UK. "I go love *o*," Àdùnní teased me often, but I didn't mind.

Mofẹ́ had told his mother he wanted to marry me and suggested that the parents have lunch so they could officially meet. Our mothers had become phone friends over the years, and Témì had even let it slip once or twice that she heard them discussing wedding colours.

"Babe, let our parents meet without us so that they can

fast-track the entire process. I want to come to Nigeria so that we can conclude arrangements before you go for the National Youth Service," Mofẹ́ suggested one night.

"I agree. Why don't we suggest they do it next week? My dad will help to convince my mum."

The day after they returned home from visiting Mofẹ́'s parents, I dropped by for dinner. "Daddy, how did it go?"

"It went well, Ládùn! Are you the first person to fall in love?" my mother answered for both of them.

"They will come for an official introduction when Mofẹ́ is back in Nigeria," my father added.

Summer came, but Mofẹ́ did not. "Baby, I am trying to get a job in London. Once that is sorted, I'll fly down," he said the day after he was meant to land in Lagos.

"Don't worry; you will get it," I said, concealing my disappointment.

A month later, Mofẹ́'s calls came less and less frequently.

He blamed his new job, complaining about how demanding it was. I was researching my final-year project, so I was also busy. In my mind, Mofẹ́'s parents would come for the official introduction whenever he returned, so I didn't let it bother me.

When I saw on Facebook a few weeks later that the Mofẹ́ whom I had spoken with was married, I was certain it was a lie. I kept calling. He kept hiding. Àdùnní tried to reach him as well, but he was unavailable. So I spoke about it with my parents on one of my weekend visits. "Daddy, I am not sure why Mofẹ́'s number is not working. I saw a prank about him being married."

"Ládùn, please leave your father alone," my mother quickly cut in.

"Mum, my husband-to-be is not reachable. I should be concerned." It sounded like I was protesting, but it was a cry for help.

"I am sure there is a reason. Give it time," my father reassured me.

I wasn't sure if this was confidence or apathy speaking. But my parents' deflection did little to assuage my fears.

I didn't stop trying. I even sent messages to his friends, but no one replied. I went on Facebook again to look at the collage of pictures. Mofẹ́ had his arms around a young woman in each one. Their smiles were so wide that their eyes were slits on their faces. The caption described her as the love of his life. Another woman, the love of his life? I commented on the last picture in the post. In it, Mofẹ́ was captured swinging his new bride in the air. "Mofẹ́, so you are married?" I commented. He blocked me immediately.

When university lecturers went on strike at the beginning of my last semester, my academic career plunged into uncertainty. I was stuck at home, miserable and ashamed that I was hoping Mofẹ́ would come back to me. I was also worried about spending an extra year in school. Témì sensed my despair and tried to take my mind off the situation. "Ládùn, don't worry. Mofẹ́ is working hard to take care of you."

"Thank you, Témì. Go and chill with your friends." How could I tell her what I had seen on Facebook?

JUMMAI IS PLENTY

*I knew they called people like me òròbò—excess everything, ev-*erywhere. "You are not fat, Jummai; you are enough," Hassana used to say to me whenever I bought a blouse but struggled to get it on. I didn't really care about my size; I loved myself. However, do not call me fat to my face, or you will face my wrath.

"Aunty Jummai, you can't be buying what Aunty Hassana is buying *now*," Ríssí, who ran a thrift store, said one day when I tried on a similar top to Hassana's. I dropped the top. She sold me ugly, baggy clothes instead. Of course, I paid Ríssí back for daring to call me fat by selling her expired provisions at a discount from Mama's shop. She nearly died. My mother beat me when she found out what I had done. "You are such an evil child, Jummai!" she screamed, whipping me with kòbóko. Mama was a slight woman and also very short, so if I wanted to fight back, I could have. However, if I did and the news got out, I would have to spend at least two weeks on my knees, begging every member of her Market Women Association, convincing them that I was not trying to kill Ríssí. I took the beating. I saw Hassana run to stop her, but I was already fainting from the pain. It was worth it, though. I taught Ríssí a lesson.

After that incident, I tried to lie low. That turned out to be an exercise in futility, as randy men wouldn't leave me be. I didn't want anyone touching me. When one of Mama's customers spanked my backside one evening, I was in a quandary. *Should I break his fingers, or slap him until sense returns to him?* He took my silence as consent, and he tried to do it again. I broke at least three of his fingers. Mama banned me from coming to her shop after that. I preferred to stay at home anyway. Apart from my grades at school, the only thing Mama complimented me on was my cooking. I also got the chance to read romance novels in peace. I couldn't have read those in front of Mama, as she would have ripped the books from end to spine. She said the pictures of men and women in the throes of passion on the covers made the books demonic. I could travel the world through books and only come out when it was time to do chores or go to school.

To me, Mama was an annoying puzzle. On the one hand, I knew she had little tolerance for men, because she always blamed my father for every ill luck that came her way. But on the other hand, even when she encouraged us to read, she never failed to add, "But don't let the books give you voices your husbands may consider too loud."

"Yes, ma," we would chorus.

Mama loved to buy me motivational books. "Jummai, read this book. It will teach you about what anger does to people."

"Thank you, ma." I never read the books Mama bought me.

Hassana didn't like to read, but she didn't mind me reading to her. Reading together kept us connected.

Hassana would come to my side of the room and lie down. As

I played with her long hair, I would read to her, my ears listening for Mama's footsteps. At the end of every novel, we would debate which characters we liked the most while eating donkwa. I was drawn to the romantic heroes, while Hassana was always invested in the plot.

"This part makes my heart break," Hassana would say.

"Heartbreak ke? We're reading about a hot man, and you're focused on whose heart he's breaking? Go and read the motivational books then. Be like your mother!" I responded.

"Shhhhh. Jummai, she will hear you. And besides, you're just like her." Hassana would cover her mouth but laugh with her eyes. I enjoyed how different we were back then. That version of Hassana understood me. Those days were long gone now.

Once she completed secondary school, Hassana opened a shop with the money Mama gifted her. She decided she was not going to further her education. She batted her lashes, and Mama let her have her way. That was when we started to drift apart. We had a pact to be together for life and sail through everything. She broke it. As payback, I applied to a university outside of Lagos. "I am filling out my form. I am going to the University of Ilorin," I announced.

"Ilorin? Jummai, we agreed that you would stay in Lagos for university education."

"And we agreed that you would go to school with me, but just look at you. Why will you make such a decision with Mama?" I opened my hands to her as if I expected the answers to drop into my palms. She stood watching as I sashayed away into the room we shared.

At the University of Ilorin, I was a beauty queen. Toasters swamped around me, and from the first day I moved into the hostel, I had help with even the littlest chore. At the market, they added extra to my goods.

"Aunty Jummai, see how I am adding járá," Súlè the meat seller would say, licking his lips.

"Add some more. Do you think one extra piece of meat is what made me like this?" I'd turn around to give him a better view.

In class, I received free materials for my difficult courses, and it was an all-around blessing that I never had to struggle. But as much as I enjoyed the attention, sometimes I wished I could put my fingers in the eyes of these men and scrub them clean of the lust they did little to hide.

When I left home, I promised myself that I would stay in Ilorin until I finished university. I also stopped reading novels and eating donkwa. They reminded me too much of Hassana. To be honest, despite the attention from men, my first year was filled with loneliness. Hassana wrote me letters, but I burnt each one without reading them. I needed something to distract me from the vacuum Hassana left in my life, so I joined the student union. That was how I met my husband.

We met at a rally. He was calmly seated amidst the chaos,

watching as the union executives screamed at the tops of their lungs.

"We no go gree."

"We will go into the classrooms and drag the lecturers out!"

Chairs were lifted, and they broke into songs that expressed their desire to end corruption in the university and secure a better life for students. He just sat there and wrote, totally detached from all the movement and noise. It was as if the other members knew better than to rile him, because they caused a ruckus everywhere except for where he sat.

"Please, who is that guy?" I asked the lady next to me. We were tightly packed in the hall, so there was no way to move forward and introduce myself.

"That's the student union president. His name is Ahmed Ayinde, but they call him Observation."

"Observation?"

"Yes, that's his nickname. He is the one that writes letters to the press and the university. He is known for using the word 'observe' a lot in his letters." I wondered if the lady was his girlfriend.

"Are you his sister?"

"No *o*, I am just a member who admires the student union government."

From the way her eyes undressed all the men at the front of the room, she was open to more than just admiration. Shameless human. A loud voice broke into my thoughts, chanting slogans.

"The greatest gbògbò! The greatest gbàgbà! Greeeeeeeeee-aaaattttt!"

I squeezed through the crowd, inhaling their smells, as I made my way to Observation. I stood directly in front of him and smiled. He looked at me, and I knew I had found my husband.

Observation pursued me for half the school year before I gave in.

"Jummai, I love you," he sang in my ears whenever we met. I could see it in his eyes that he truly cared for me.

"You say that now, but what if you leave me?" I would retort.

"I will never, ever leave you. You are the one for me."

I agreed to be his woman at the end of that semester. Observation became my Hassana.

I enjoyed the fact that he was a notorious troublemaker for the university management. To avoid getting arrested easily, he stayed off campus. Cooking was my love language, so I would go to his house every weekend, cook, and even offer to sleep over.

"No, Jummai. Please go to your hostel," he said whenever I tried to initiate lovemaking.

In my second year, I succeeded in seducing Ahmed. We made love in the classroom where I studied at night while other students were sleeping. He was seated beside me, but his mind had wandered off. He feigned ignorance when I slipped my hand up his thigh to his zipper. I ran my finger along it, hoping to get a reaction like I had read in books. His penis twitched, and Observation looked up. "Jummai, what are . . ."

I put a finger to his lips. "No one is watching."

His mouth opened, and a smile danced around his lips. I pulled him out, and I used my other hand to pull my leggings down. I sat astride him and sank slowly onto him. Soon we had to cover each other's mouths, and then something happened. I saw stars, and Observation convulsed. I had fucked him to make him mine. After that, we were inseparable. We were in love, and he was my family. When Observation graduated, he lobbied to be posted to our campus for his year of national service.

In my final year, he asked me to marry him. I said yes. I wanted to go back home with a husband *and* a degree so I could rub them in Hassana's face. By the time I got back from Ilorin, Hassana had moved to Ilé-Ifè with Mama.

At least they attended my wedding in Lagos. Mama and Hassana sat far away from Ahmed's family, only interacting with those that walked over to greet them. Shioor! Even on my wedding day, Mama could not put aside our issues to present a united front for my in-laws.

When Mama passed away, I thought the only problematic person I knew in life was gone, until Observation showed me who he truly was.

HASSANA'S FACE

Growing up, I believed it was my duty to be beautiful, if only as the fulfillment of my name. From a young age, I saw that my breasts were different from Jummai's. While hers stood like they were ready to fight their owner, mine were gentle and shy. Yes, we both had backsides that made other young girls envious, but I was intimidated by Jummai's. In fact, on days when people didn't remark on my beauty and my body, I went home to bathe and dress again, then rub some of Mama's shea butter on my skin. When I stepped out, I would walk through the usual places where they sang my praises and wait, pretending to be busy with a novel.

"Hassana, you are looking beautiful this evening."

"Hassana, your skin is magic. Please share your secrets."

"Hassana, you are special."

"It is only a big man that can marry you."

It was only then that my day would start. I had received the validation I needed from my admirers.

✳

When we were younger, Wednesday was my favourite day of the week. I woke up excited because after school, Mama Jubril, the woman who lived down the street, would bring her freshly made donkwa to Mama's shop. Once it clocked three p.m., I would run out of the store and wait, watching her walk lazily down the muddy street, until she got to our store. The wooden box on her head would be gracefully balanced, its transparent glass showing the donkwa, groundnut, and popcorn.

"Hassana, my favourite customer!"

"Good afternoon, ma." I would smile brightly at the compliment.

When I handed her some money, she would pack the appropriate amount into a square of old newspaper before placing the donkwa box back on her head. Mama Jubril would continue her walk through the market, and I would run back in and draw Jummai out of whatever world the book she was reading had pulled her into. "Come and eat donkwa. It is still warm."

"I don't know why we buy snacks from that woman whose nails are always black with dirt."

"She washed her hands today."

"How do you know?"

"I asked her to show them to me."

Jummai would look up at me. "Liar, liar." She'd point her fingers at me in an accusatory manner.

"I am not lying," I would say, slicing the donkwa. I would hold the bigger half out to her. As usual, she took it only after eyeing it suspiciously, and then once she put it in her mouth, she would inhale the rest of the snack so quickly that I almost never had more than the half I ate to convince her. After that, she'd read to me my favourite stories from the books we loved. We were happy back then.

As we grew older, the differences between Jummai and my mother became more obvious. I tried to always find a way for them to live in peace with each other. My mother, on the other hand, was Jummai's nemesis.

The first time she hit Jummai was the day Jummai sold expired provisions to Ríssí. It nearly cost Mama one of her shops, because she was reported to the Ìyá Olójà, leader of the Market Women Association. Mama had to bribe people to plead on her behalf. She had almost beaten Jummai to death by the time I got home. Thankfully, I arrived just in time and took Jummai to the nearest clinic.

"If she wants to die, let her die," Mama said when the doctor came to see us the next day. I knew she didn't mean it. I had seen the fear in her eyes when Jummai collapsed. I made a vow with Jummai later that evening. "Let us not beat our children, Jummai."

"I hope your mother dies," she mumbled through swollen lips.

"Don't say that. She is your mother too, and she asked me to give you some provisions."

"If you leave them here, I will trash them." Jummai looked away.

"Jummai, the one with the heart of gold. Look at me."

"I don't want anything from her."

I knew she was still angry, but she accepted Mama's peace offering because *I* was the messenger. When the market women heard about our mother nearly killing Jummai, the Ìyá Olójà decided to let sleeping dogs lie.

After secondary school, I quit formal education. The letters on the blackboard and in books wouldn't stay in place as I struggled to make sense of the words. I would try to catch them with my eyes and my hands, but they escaped me. "Mama, please let me go to baking school. Everyone in Lagos likes cake now. I have been told that I don't understand words."

She was hesitant, but after I refused to eat for two days, she gave in and sent me to baking school. "Hassana, I didn't go to school, but I made something out of myself. You can at least start life with your WASSCE results."

"Thank you, Mama." I knelt before her. When I stood up, I saw Jummai in the doorway. Her eyes were red, so I followed her. "Jummai, please try to understand. School is hard for me."

"I will help you. We will go to the same university and study the same course, in the same year. I will write your exams for you. Just don't leave me."

"I will always come to visit you. School is not for me."

She ignored me and focused on the novel in her hand. And that was how our relationship turned sour. I tried to appease her, but no one held a grudge like Jummai. Once she finished secondary school a year later, she took entrance examinations for the University of Ilorin to spite me.

I was busy with baking school, so I was able to avoid Jummai's wrath during the day, but at night, she didn't speak to me, even though we shared a room. Within a month, I had everyone eating my pastries, and my teachers sang my praises. All the men forgot about the ingredients and just looked at me. It was easy for me to be at the top. The thing about being beautiful was that people listened to you. They favoured you.

"Hassana, your ìkébè will be the death of me," the head of transportation in Lagos, my latest admirer, said to me as he drove me home from the academy. I basked in the attention. It was better than the daggers in Jummai's eyes. I came back one day, and Jummai had left for Ilorin. It was just me and my mother. She started teaching me how to prepare to move into my husband's house.

"I don't want to marry any of these men; they don't love me," I wanted to tell her, but her excitement was contagious. She showed me how to serve my husband and how to bathe her future grand-children.

After baking school, I'd saved enough money to open a bake-shop on Allen Avenue, Ìkejà. I wanted to be far from my mother's stores on Lagos Island. Business was thriving, although I had more male customers than female. I baked different flavours of cakes and other small pastries.

The first time Atiku visited my bakeshop, I was out for lunch. My shop assistant, who doubled as the manager, took down his order absentmindedly. I ended up baking a vanilla sponge cake even though he had ordered a chocolate cake for his mother's six-tieth birthday.

"Good afternoon. I have come to pick up the cake I ordered."

"Good afternoon, sir. Please, what is the name on your order?" I didn't look up as I flipped open the hardback notebook labelled "Orders."

"Atiku Haruna."

Even though the words floated, I located his entry in a few minutes. I went to the back and brought his cake out. "Happy birthday to your mum," I said, handing the cake box to him.

He lifted the cover. "The perfect chocolate cake. Mum will love this. Thank you."

"Chocolate cake? You ordered vanilla, sir."

"No, I ordered chocolate cake."

"No, sir. Vanilla is what is written here." I inched closer to him. He smelled like incensed wood burning in a warm, friendly fire.

"No, I said chocolate, but I noticed the salesgirl was very busy that day. She must have made a mistake. My mother hates vanilla."

I flipped through the book again to check if the manager had made alterations that I had missed on the order. He had paid twelve thousand naira for the cake. I made a profit of five thousand. If I remade the cake, I wouldn't break even.

He sighed. "I am willing to pay extra if you can please bake it again, miss, or is it missus?"

I looked at him. "Miss Abdallah," a title my new boyfriend, Israel, was looking to change. He had already asked to see my mother twice.

I met Israel by accident. I wanted to buy fish for our evening meal, but the fish seller was not at his usual spot in the market.

"Aah, my fine aunty, he has travelled for Sallah," the fishmonger's neighbour seller informed me. She stood outside her shop of soup items. "There is a place that just opened down the street, and they sell different kinds of fish. The owner is a young man."

The shop was about to close when I got there. "Please, I would like to buy Titus."

"We only have Panla," the shopkeeper answered. He looked too young to be the owner of the shop, with his low-riding jeans and a vest flung over his shoulders. He held one wing of the door open, dragging a log of wood from a corner to stop it from slamming shut. "I know you. You are the fine girl that bakes. I even want to start eating sugar because of you."

I found his forwardness endearing. We quickly became friends.

He was hardworking, funny, and had a polytechnic certificate. His fish business was doing really well, and I knew he would make me happy.

"Hassana, if you marry me, you won't regret it," Israel blurted a few months into our friendship.

I chuckled. "Israel, I have not even agreed to date you, and you're talking about marriage."

"You will marry me. You are my wife."

"I will pay an extra fifteen thousand, Miss Abdallah." Atiku's voice brought me back from my reverie.

"Don't worry, it's on the house. Please recommend our business to your friends."

"I'll be sure to do that." He smiled shyly. "I hope I'm not too forward, but are you Hausa?"

"Yes, I am, but I am more Yoruba than Hausa." Sometimes I forgot that I was Hausa because I didn't speak much of the language anymore. It helped me forget that my father had left us. My mother sharpened her tongue the Lagos way, but her pointed nose and beautiful long hair betrayed her.

"You are quite popular; everyone likes your cake." His brown eyes seemed to change to black as he leaned over the counter. His long lashes, pointed nose, and pink lips complemented his bald head; he smiled briefly, and I knew he was trying to charm me. Otherwise, why offer to pay extra and not shout at the baker?

"Do you own this shop?"

"I will start working on the cake now, and you can pick it up early tomorrow." I was not interested in talking further with him.

"Why don't you deliver it?"

"I don't do deliveries, sir."

"I'll pay extra, and please, call me Atiku. I am only thirty-one."

"Okay, Atiku."

"I will add an extra five thousand."

"Okay. What's the address?"

"8B Ìkòyí Boulevard."

"I will be there at seven a.m." I wanted him to leave.

"See you tomorrow, then." He handed me his complimentary card and left.

I got Israel to drive me very early the next day because I wanted Atiku to know I had a boyfriend. I delivered the cake, declined his invitation to stay for the party, and went back to my shop.

My birthday was the following week, and Israel was planning a trip to Ghana.

"I hope you will let me taste you, Hassana. I am hungry."

"You will taste me after you see my mother."

"This woman."

"Israel, I won't go on this trip with you if your plan is to sleep with me. In fact, you must give me the money for my plane ticket before we leave."

"Trust me. I won't touch you now, but when we marry, I will show you. These—your thick thighs—will not rest," he teased, and I laughed at him as he growled. With his dreadlocks tied in a knot above his head, he wiggled his bushy eyebrows and winked. He towered over me, and I enjoyed tracing the patterns on the batik shirts he usually favoured.

My mother allowed me to go with him. I think age softened her.

"Since you are not going to university, you might as well find a man that can give you babies. He may eventually turn out to be useless, but you will have your children and your business."

"Okay, Mama."

"Just be careful. Don't sleep with him until he marries you. Also, hold on to your money as you go on this journey."

"Okay."

It was on that trip that Israel proposed to me, and I agreed to be his wife. We got to know each other even better. Israel's Yoruba name was Olumide, but he went by his Christian name. He didn't use his local names—his identity card said Israel T. King.

"People do business with you when they can't place where you are from," Israel argued.

"Israel, this is one Nigeria."

"Hassana, I know you are smarter than that *now*. Which one

Nigeria? Does Abacha look like a head of state that preaches one Nigeria?"

"You know I don't read newspapers."

"That is not something to be proud of. I will send you to university once we marry. My wife must be sound academically."

I didn't mention the letters running away from me. He was a fish seller, and I a baker. *How was school supposed to help us in our businesses?* I wondered.

After my birthday trip, Atiku started to pursue me in earnest. I had never seen that kind of consistency. Most men chase, and after a month, they burn out. Atiku was after me for six months, even when he knew Israel had been to see my mother. He showered me with gifts, offered to open a new shop for me, and made Mama fall in love with him. He told her he wanted to marry me. It was obvious she preferred him to Israel.

"Mama, Israel has already come to see you," I protested after she brought up the matter of my possible marriage to Atiku.

"Please, I don't know what you are talking about."

"I have a husband already, ma."

"Keep quiet! Atiku is from a powerful family. I sell provisions, you bake cakes, Israel sells fish, so you marry him and become what? Ìyàwó Ẹléja? Atiku is from a political family. If you marry him, he will give us dignity. Marriage is not about love."

I didn't argue with her. Since Jummai left, I tried to be at peace with Mama. I suspected she missed her usual spats with Jummai, but I was not the type to trade words with anyone. Whenever I felt the combative mood enter the house with her, I hid in my room or went over to Israel's house.

One evening, while Israel was away in Ògbómòshó scouting for bigger fish farms, my mother decided to travel to her village.

"I am going for a few days. I want to see my family. I have been having dreams about them."

"Can I come, Mama?"

"No, you stay here. They are not good people. I don't want their eyes on you."

I was by myself when Atiku visited my shop and invited me to his house.

"No," I repeated for the umpteenth time.

"My mother wants to meet you."

"I said no!"

"Hassana, please." Atiku fell to his knees and held on to my ankle. I gave in.

The gate of the Haruna residence resembled a lion's mouth, as if to warn visitors that they were entering at their own risk. Atiku pressed a button on the remote control he had in his car and it opened, cutting the ferocious beast into two halves. Their home was like a palace, and the upholstered furniture was adorned with gold paint. Alhaja, his mother, was waiting in the living room when we arrived.

"Our beautiful wife," she said, her eyes travelling over my face.

"Good evening, ma."

Alhaja patted the cushion of the two-seater she lounged on. "Come and sit beside me."

I went to her, but I didn't relax into her embrace.

"You must eat something."

"I am fine, ma."

"Nonsense! The cook has prepared a feast. Why don't you join me at the dining table?" She had a heavy northern accent.

I intended to stay only a few minutes, but the food relaxed me, as did the stories of Atiku's youth that his mother told. I sneaked a glance at my wristwatch. "I should get going, ma."

"My dear, it's late. There will be soldiers patrolling all the major roads. It's not safe. You know how they can be."

She was right.

"Sleep here, and Atiku will drop you at home tomorrow."

Atiku led me down a long hallway and opened the last door on the left. It was a large room, and it smelt like incensed wood. He threw my bag onto the armchair beside his bed and wrapped his arms around me. He pressed his lips on mine.

I knew I wasn't ready to be with him. I had promised Israel that he would be my first. Atiku peeled my clothes off even as I protested. "Atiku, stop! Please stop. Your mother is downstairs."

"Shhhhh. My mother wants us to be together. She says you are my wife."

My mind travelled as he started to suck my breasts.

When he forced himself into me, all I could do was whimper.

Early next day, Israel was standing outside my gate when Atiku dropped me off. As I got out of the car and walked toward him, Israel took off in the opposite direction.

I ran inside the house, threw my things in my room, and rushed to Israel's home, plagued with guilt. I confessed what had happened, hoping he would be sympathetic. Israel broke up with me instantly, despite my pleas. I stayed on my knees and he just ignored me, busying himself with cleaning. My sniffles and repeated explanations seemed to further harden his heart.

"When you are ready, lock the door behind you. I am going out," he said after a while.

I wanted to run to the door of his one-bedroom flat to stop him from leaving, but I decided to let him have his space.

Atiku made several attempts to see me, but I had escaped to my aunty's house in Mushin. I needed a change of scenery. I baked from her house and sent the goods to the shop. If Jummai was still talking to me, I would have paid her a visit. She hadn't responded to any of my letters, so I wrote to her again:

My dear Àbúrò,

I miss U. Many tins av happened to me. I lost my flower to a wicked man. I want to come to ur skul. Please send hostel number and adress.

I love U.

I took it to the motor park and gave it to Bàbá Múrí. "Daddy, are you sure you give her my letters?"

"Ahn ahn, is it not that your sister that is full; she resemble you but she short? Aunty Hassana, I dey give am."

"Please give her this one and tell her to reply."

"Okay, my fine aunty."

I stayed in Mushin for two weeks. My aunt and her family took care of me.

"It is not every day we have royalty in our midst," she said as she served me àmàlà and okro with beef on my first night.

"Aunty, I can't finish it."

"You must eat. My sister doesn't feed you enough."

I noticed I was starting to put on weight because of all the meals and her refusal to let me lift a finger. I moved back home. Two weeks was enough time to cool off, so I looked for Israel in Obálèndé, but he had left Lagos.

"Ma, please, do you know anyone I can reach from his family?" I asked his landlady.

"Hassana, Israel doesn't have a family. He moved here and rented the house on his own."

I felt my tummy turn, but I kept a smile on my face. Where could he have gone to, and how did he move on so soon? "If you see him, ma, please tell him I am looking for him."

"No problem, I am sure he will be back. He is your husband; he can't leave you."

I knew she meant well, but her words mocked my aching heart. I was broken, and I knew it. Israel hated me. I stopped baking altogether and settled in Mushin. I really didn't want to see Atiku. He left many letters that my mother sent to me, but I burnt them all, unopened.

Finally, the letters stopped.

"He came to tell me he is moving to another country and I should tell you goodbye. I don't know how you lost two men suddenly, Hassana. That is a thing I expect from Jummai," my mother said to me when she came to Mushin.

I returned home with Mama, feeling very lost, until I met Tító.

I never told my mother what Atiku did to me. She was a great businesswoman, but she devoted too much time to nursing her hatred for my father. That fury chased away her suitors. My mother was a handsome woman, and she would have complemented any man. Perhaps she didn't want anyone because her womb was also exhausted.

"Look at me. I don't need a man. If any man comes to me, I will curse him."

Not all days were bad. Whenever Mama's friends visited, they would reminisce about their childhood, and she would become animated, throwing her gèlè on the floor, and untying her wrapper as she danced with passion. On those days, her lunch was ofàdà rice and seven pieces of orisirisi, and I would serve èko and moin-moin for dinner. Most days, however, were spent walking on eggshells around her.

"Hassana! Have you hung the clothes outside? Don't waste the sun today like you did yesterday. Dry the clothes and the pepper before I come back. Otherwise, you and I will wear the same trouser!"

After I'd closed my own shop, Mama told me to supervise the five service girls that worked in her stores in Ìsàlè Èkó.

"I don't want them to get too comfortable and steal my money."

The Ifẹ̀/Modákéké war of 1997 brought Titó to me in Lagos, as he had to abandon his home for a few months. The university had also shut down. I would later find out his mother, Ìyá Agba, had been killed, and he needed to get away to grieve properly. The war did a lot of damage, because when two elephants fight, it is the grass that suffers, so the indigenes of both towns, Ilé-Ifẹ̀ and Modákéké, lost loved ones and properties.

"No one knows why two neighbouring towns in the same state would be enemies. The people of Modákéké claim they have always felt like strangers and are disrespected," he shared with me.

It was as if the universe knew I needed a saviour. Titó came to my mother's shop for provisions.

"Good afternoon. Please, do you have Cowbell milk, Milo, Cabin Biscuit, and some ginger tea?"

His throaty voice made me look up, and his appearance did not fit the voice. I expected to see a grump, but his face was kind.

"We do. How much do you want?"

"As much as you can give me, Aunty." I heard the joke in his voice.

I handed him the goods and got back to trying to read the newspaper.

He started coming to the shop regularly, and soon we became friends. We married a month after we met.

"Hassana, I want to marry you."

"Titó, you don't know me. I am not who you think I am."

"I know enough. I will follow you anywhere. I can even move to Lagos and teach at a university here."

His words fanned my face, and we inhaled the same air. Tító wasn't handsome in a conventional way, but he was nice-looking. His face had deep smile lines that ran from each side of his nose to his mouth, and his lower-middle teeth overlapped. He was a foot taller, so I felt protected. He wasn't like Atiku or Israel; he was comfortable with my silence. He didn't push me; he accepted me as I was. I had nothing to offer Tító, but he was fine with it. I moved to live with him in Ilé-Ifẹ̀ and chose to find peace in anonymity. Ilé-Ifẹ̀ was not Lagos; everyone moved at a pace that favoured them rather than running after time like mad people. I wrote to Jummai about my decision even though I knew a response might never come.

Jummai,

I have found peace. His name is Tító. I am moving to Ilé-Ifẹ̀with him. Mama says she will come along with me, so she is selling her business.

I love u. I pray u come back home before I marry.

Tító showed me his family home, or what was left of it. His mother had been burnt to death in the house during the war.

"They burnt people and their houses, Hassana. Do you understand why I prefer to live on campus?"

I nodded solemnly. "I understand."

"I couldn't even be there to save my mother."

Titó took care of me. During the early days of our marriage, he helped me with my dyslexia. We read books together, saying the words aloud slowly. Soon I was able to read and write properly on my own. He loved me openly and without apology.

"I will start giving you pocket money, Hassana. I know you have savings from your business, but as my wife, I will give you something for yourself, aside from the monthly bills."

He let the world know I was his wife.

Mama died in Ifẹ̀, six months later. I think she was waiting for one of her children to find a home before answering the call of her ancestors. I forgot about baking and settled into my new life. I am glad I made that decision, because Abacha's regime became more chaotic, and a year later, he was allegedly murdered.

Lagos reminds me of my pain, yet that is where Ládùn and Témì want to call home. Children are wicked.

part three

OMOLÁDÙN AYÉ AND HER FIVE YEARS

HASSANA'S CHILDREN

Omoládùn came into the world the day after Titó's birthday in 1997. She refused to open her eyes until Titó cut the umbilical cord that joined us. It was as if she knew her father was with her, even at birth. Even then she didn't seem too comfortable with me. Once she was able to walk, she started following her father everywhere. Whenever he left her with me, she would cry for hours until I gave up and wept too.

"Ládùn is so strong-willed. I don't think we need to have another child," Titó said one day during their afternoon game of hide-and-seek.

"Please don't talk like that; we are having another baby."

Their bond became so tight that I had Témìnikan four years later so that I too would have a friend. We named her Témìladé, but I know her name is Témìnikan because I wanted a child that could love me the way Titó and Ládùn loved each other. She is the child that chose me. My own.

I can recall many instances when that Ládùn girl has shown me that my feelings don't matter to her. For example, I asked Témì and Ládùn to call me Màámi. I like that title more than Mummy;

it sounds more personal. I heard Ìyá Malik's children call her that, and my insides melted.

"I prefer Mummy," Ládùn responded quietly.

"Why are you so stubborn?" I retorted.

"Don't worry, Màámi. I'll call you whatever you like," Témì said cheerfully, making it impossible for me to stay angry. I complained to Titó when he returned from work.

"Baby, please let her call you what she likes," he said to me.

"I knew you would support her. Your child doesn't like me."

"Ládùn loves you. You and she will get closer as she grows older."

"I should wait till then? The girl acts as if she doesn't know me. I carried her in my womb, yet she treats me like a stranger."

Ládùn and Titó were inseparable. They celebrated their birthdays together, and she often went with him to the farm where we grew most of our food. At first, the four of us all went together. But Témì, after the first visit, had a severe allergic reaction to grass, so I stayed at home with her. Secretly, I didn't care for the farming either.

On one of their farming trips, Ládùn and her father came home with sacks of corn, pear, and cocoa. The bags filled with farm produce dragged in by Ládùn left a trail of dirt on the kitchen floor as Titó took their farming equipment into the shed behind the house.

"Good morning, Mummy." Ládùn knelt to greet me.

"Good morning, ma," I responded. Would it be so hard to call me Màámi?

Témì grabbed a broom and started to sweep after her sister. "Ládùn, see how you are giving me work now!"

"Sorry, please help me." She turned and tried to hug her sister.

"Ewww. Go and baff." Témì dodged her, and Ládùn headed for the bathroom they shared, leaving the sack near the pantry.

"Ládùn, after your shower, I want to show you a book about that Dongo yaro plant we spoke about earlier," Tító called out from the backyard.

"Okay, Daddy." Ládùn smiled.

"Baby, I am really hungry. Help me cook some corn quickly," Tító said to me as he walked toward our bedroom.

"Okay, love." I rose from the three-seater where I watched the antics of my children. I rushed into the kitchen, rinsed the corn-cobs, and placed them in a large pot. Half an hour later, I brought one out to taste. The cob was halfway to my mouth when Ládùn snuck up on me.

"Mummy, don't eat my daddy's corn until he comes out. Daddy! Mummy is eating our corn."

"Ahn ahn, Aunty Ládùn! It is everybody's corn. Besides, I am only tasting it for your father so that it is soft enough."

She walked over with her hands stretched out. "Give me, I will taste it for him."

"As how?"

"It is only the people that farm that should eat first from the produce. Others can eat after."

I was too stunned to speak, so I handed the corn over and left the kitchen.

"Daddy, our corn is ready. Témì, come and take corn!" she called out.

I walked into our bedroom and watched as Titó looked through his books on the shelf opposite our bed. He had just taken a shower, so the room smelt of freshly plucked mint leaves.

"Baby, is the corn ready?" he asked, without looking at me.

"Your child has sent me away from the kitchen, saying since I did not farm, I should not eat the food you brought. So please go and ask your daughter if it's ready," I said in a huff.

He threw his head back and laughed at me. "Come, baby, let us go and eat. I am sure she was just joking. She's only ten."

That was it. No reprimanding the girl for being so disrespectful. Later that day, Témì fed me some more corn as we sat to watch television. I nibbled on it grudgingly. Ládùn and her father had gone to bed.

"Eat corn, Màámi. Don't mind Ládùn. We will start our own farm here, but we will use fake grass," she said as she chewed noisily.

Over the years, I watched Ládùn and Titó's bond grow deeper. I might have been a little jealous, but that was the side of me that wished I had a father like Titó too.

Ládùn was Titó's world, and so when she asked us to meet Mofẹ́'s parents, her father agreed, despite my reservations. "Where I am from, the man's parents make the first move."

"Baby, please let's just go. Ládùn really loves him. Let's do this for her."

"They are the ones that should come and meet us, Titó. What kind of thing is this?"

"Sweetheart, Mofẹ́'s father is always away on business, but now that he's around, let's just go so they know we are friendly. Besides, we can take a small vacation. I need you to stop being afraid of Lagos."

"This is wrong. Tradition everywhere demands that the groom's parents come to the bride's home, not the other way around. My Ládùn is too beautiful for this nonsense."

"Calm down. It's just lunch. They will come over for a proper introduction before Mofẹ́ and Ládùn get married. I am sure they are people who respect culture."

The day we were to meet Mofẹ́'s parents arrived with a light rain shower. I woke up feeling nervous. I had not been to Lagos in a long time, and I didn't want to go there not looking my best. Lagos welcomes everyone but allows a select few to survive. And those survivors have to be on their A game always. I didn't want Lagos to think I hadn't done well just because it had spat me out. So we woke up early and washed the car together. I wore the new aso-òkè gown that Titó had bought for me on my last birthday. Titó was dressed in a batik shirt and black trousers. We were determined to impress our future in-laws. Témì was in Ládùn's hostel for the weekend, and Jummai stayed at home by herself.

We played Ebenezer Obey until we got to Lagos, singing to each other:

> Kò sí Ogbón tó le da
> Kò sí wà to le wu
> To lè fi táyé Lórùn o

They gave us an address that was difficult to locate. It didn't help that those we asked sent us on a merry-go-round.

"My good man, please, could you show us the way to Ogbà?" Tító asked a man dressed in a greasy green jumper, who was seated by the side of the road near his tyre-fixing machine. He looked grateful for a conversation to distract him from the scorching sun and the absence of customers.

"You have missed the road, sir. Turn back, take left, take right, then the second turn at the roundabout."

"Thank you so much."

"Anytime. Find something for me *now*, my brother." He rubbed his hands together and smiled.

Tító looked through the glove compartment and fished out a crisp two hundred naira note, which he handed over.

"Lagos has not changed," I said to him as we followed the instructions. We ended up getting lost again. We called our future in-laws in a final cry for help, and they sent their driver to lead us to their house. We got to their home and were ushered into a duplex whose exterior belied the owners' opulence. The off-white walls and gleaming hardwood floors made me feel at ease. I liked the house. We waited downstairs.

"Baby, this place is beautiful," Tító whispered as we settled into the three-seater in the living room that was big enough to seat twenty.

"I know, right? I hope Mofẹ́ works as hard as his parents so that our daughter is well taken care of."

"Baby . . ."

Our conversation was cut short by the sound of our hosts'

laughter. We looked up, and two figures emerged from a door to the right, and we stood to greet them. Mofẹ́'s father looked uncomfortably familiar, but there are stories that the man upstairs creates us all in twos and threes, then scatters us across the face of the earth, so I didn't flinch.

"Our in-laws, welcome. It is so good to finally put faces to Ládùn's parents." Mofẹ́'s mother smiled as she touched my arm lightly. "My name is Lola, and this is my husband, Israel Tówojú. He is called the fish man."

The ground shook beneath me, and I held Titó's hand tightly for support.

Titó looked at me briefly. "Thank you for inviting us to your home. This is my wife, Hassana. I am Titó. We are so happy to meet the people who raised Mofẹ́."

Israel said nothing, but I could feel his eyes boring holes into the top of my head as I stared at my feet. "We are pleased to meet you as well. Are we not, honey?" Lola said, nudging Israel with her elbow.

"I know Hassana. Sweetheart, this is the Hassana who I told you cheated on me with another man while we were engaged."

Silence.

Titó sighed, and the mood changed like a bolt of lightning. "Well, Israel, now that we are going to be in-laws, I am sure we can move on from the past," Titó said, attempting to fill the silence. The Tówojús took a seat, and we followed suit. Titó inched closer to me, pulled me into the curve of his right arm, and rubbed the goose bumps on my arms. Their cook's footsteps broke the silence. Lola stood. "Please excuse me for a minute," she said as they left the living room.

"I am sorry, but my son and your daughter cannot be together. Ládùn is a lovely girl, but it won't work." Israel cut straight to the point.

I sank to the floor. "Israel, please . . ."

Lola returned. "Ah! What's going on here?"

"I have told them the marriage can't happen; our son won't marry their daughter."

I saw the confusion on her face.

"Darling, come on. Why would you say that? Let's go and eat, and then we can talk after."

Tító helped me up and led me to the dining table. The spread looked like the Last Supper, and the food tasted like sawdust. Tító and Lola kept the conversation going, but when Israel wasn't judging me with his eyes, he was devouring his àmàlà, ewédú, and bushmeat with gusto, catching every string of ewédú with his tongue before it dripped. After the meal, we returned to the living room.

"We know you have a list for us. Can we see it?" Lola asked. Tító grabbed my bag, fished out the bride price list, and handed it over to her. "Okay, we will be in touch. Thank you," Lola said. They led us to our car, but when we got in, it refused to start. We spent another awkward hour trying to fix it.

I cried all through the night at the hotel, and Tító just kept comforting me.

"Ládùn is going to hate me, Tító."

"She doesn't have to know."

"How do we hide this?"

"Like we have hidden everything else."

"Ládùn mentioned that Mofẹ́ looks up to his father. Israel will make sure they never get married."

"Mofẹ́ is a man. I'm sure he will tell his father to support him. He loves Ládùn, baby. They will be fine."

I didn't say anything. I just lay alone with my thoughts and wished time travel were possible. I closed my eyes to sleep, but my mind was too busy. Eventually, I decided to watch a film as Titó snored softly beside me. The film felt too close to home: it was about a married woman who lost everything when her long-lost lover reappeared and revealed all her secrets, including the fact that her first child was from another man.

The next morning, I was sullen and defeated. Titó groomed himself in front of the full-length mirror in our hotel room, continuing our conversation from the night before, like no time had passed. "Besides, why is Israel acting like a saint? Isn't Mofẹ́ older than Ládùn? This means he had a child during your relationship!"

I sat up straight. "Oh my God! You are right. So why is he behaving like this, then? Maybe he thinks Ládùn will be like me?"

"Well I certainly hope our children are like us and take each of our best sides," Titó responded, picking up our bags as we headed for the door.

"You know what I mean," I protested.

I got no response.

Two days later, I received a text from Lola. The family had no interest in their son marrying Ládùn.

I am really sorry, but my husband and I don't think your daughter is the right fit for Mofẹ́. We wish her the best of luck and hope she finds true love.

TITÓ AND I HAD JUST BEGUN SEEING EACH OTHER WHEN I FOUND out I was three months pregnant. I was much too scared to tell my mother, so I told Titó. I was ready to take it out, but he insisted that he wanted me to keep the child. "Children don't know anything about their parents' mistakes. Why should they have to bear the brunt?"

"My mother will kill me. She has put too much effort into raising me and my sister. We can't have children out of wedlock."

"Then marry me, Hassana."

"And give you another man's child?"

"No one needs to know except us. Besides, if you marry me, they will assume I married you because I got you pregnant."

"Why would you do that, Titó?"

"I love you, Hassana. I will also love our child."

"What if the child grows up and finds out? Or meets someone from their father's side?"

"We will write my name on the birth certificate and reveal the truth as soon as our child is done with university. We will keep it a secret until then."

That was it. We got married.

Titó stayed up at night, listening to Ládùn in my belly and talking to her. "My first fruit, I can't wait to meet you. I know you are a girl because your kicks are emphatic."

"Are you now a seer? What if it is a boy?"

"Please, don't call my child 'it.' She is a beautiful girl, and we will call her Omoládùn because she has brought me joy, and children really are the joy of the earth."

I kept waiting for him to change, waiting for him to treat Ládùn differently. But he was always gentle with her and corrected her with love when she was naughty. He didn't believe in flogging children. Tító may have loved her even more than his own child.

The night Ládùn found out about my history with Israel, she assailed me with many words. "Why didn't you tell me why Mofẹ́ left me? You knew what happened, and you let me walk around depressed all these months. If I hadn't called Mofẹ́'s mother, would you have even told me?" Ládùn's voice was laced with barely concealed anger.

"Ládùn, I planned to tell you, just like I planned to tell you that . . ." The words refused to leave my lips.

"Planned to tell me what? What more are you hiding from me?"

"Ládùn, that man . . . is your real father," I stuttered.

You could have heard a pin drop in the silence.

"Which man? The man you cheated on Mofẹ́'s father with?"

I whispered, "I didn't cheat."

"That is not the point! So the man is my real father?"

"Yes, Ládùn. Tító is not your biological father. We were going to tell you when—"

"Mummy, how are you able to live with yourself?"

As she continued to scream, I wondered what else she thought I could have done as a mother. Did she think I was going to break her heart by sharing such news in her final year and risk her failing her exams? Did she think I was going to tell her when I found out that Mofẹ́ had gotten married shortly after? Why are children so naïve?

There is a popular Yoruba proverb that says, *When an elder falls, he looks back; but when a child falls, he looks ahead.* I had fallen, and I had to reflect on my past so it shouldn't affect my children anymore.

"I can't live in this house with you, Mum!"

"Where are you going to go?"

"I don't know, but I'm leaving." She stalked away in the direction of her room, her phone pressed against her ear. Thirty minutes later, I heard Ládùn's bedroom door slam as she appeared, rolling a suitcase. Shortly after, her friend Àdùnní arrived in a car.

"Good evening, ma."

"Àdùnní, good evening."

"Àdùnní, wait for me in the car," Ládùn interrupted.

"This is not an American movie! Where are you going? You can't leave; it's not safe," I yelled.

Jummai came home just then, her white sutana grazing the living room rug. As usual, she had her massive Bible clutched under her arm like she couldn't hurt a fly. "What is happening? You, where are you going? And why are you talking to your mother like that?" she said, blocking Ládùn's way. Ládùn said many unkind words, which she surely didn't mean, and when I heard Jummai push back in my defence, I knew it was going to be a long night.

Ládùn ran into the kitchen and grabbed the knife that was

beside her graduation cake. She pointed it menacingly. "Aunty Jummai, move!"

"Jesu *o*!" Jummai jumped out of the way.

Ládùn picked up her suitcase and stormed out. A moment later, I heard the screech of tyres, and then there was silence. How was I to know that she would not return for five years? How was I to know that she would not forgive me?

The night Ládùn left, Tító cried like a child. He wept bitterly and tried to reach her and Àdùnní, but they didn't answer their phones. Tító blamed me for letting her go. "Why on earth would you allow our child to walk out?" It was the first time I had seen him angry with me.

"I should have stopped someone who was screaming and threatening me?"

"Yes! You should have tried to placate her!"

"Tító, I can't beg Ládùn. She was rude."

"You don't listen. We can't parent these kids this way. They are human beings; we also need to respect them."

"Don't worry; she will be back."

We tried to reach her, to no avail. Finally, when she sent a text, it was abrupt.

I can't forgive you, Mum. I need time.

That was the problem with Tító giving these girls a voice. He raised them to speak back to us. To her father, she texted,

I love you, Daddy. I will text you when I am settled.

As if I hadn't carried her for ten months and two days.

We had to tell Jummai the truth about Ládùn's biological father. She had witnessed the fight, so there was no point in hiding
it from her. I told her everything and she cried, but I was not
bothered. Her tears were years too late. She could have used that
energy to respond to one letter. Even though someone else put
her in me, Tító was Ládùn's father.

We waited for weeks to hear from Ládùn. The first week, I
thought she would come back. I called, texted, and threatened.
She blocked my number and spoke only to her father. Weeks
turned into months, and Ládùn's anger only caused mine to
grow.

What an ungrateful child she was. How many women in my
position would have done what I did for her? How many children
could boast of their fathers doing what Tító had done for Ládùn,
a child who was not his own? That man married me with a child
in my belly, covered my shame, hid me from Atiku, and this was
how Ládùn chose to repay us? That Ládùn is a wicked child. She
had a man who took her as his and looked for her even when she
strayed from home. Some of us are not so blessed.

A whole year passed, and Ládùn was still angry. Tító begged
me to go to Lagos to see her, but I refused. At least he knew where
she was.

"She is hurting, Hassana."

"So am I. Is it my fault that Israel turned out to be Mofé's
father?"

"Just try to understand. He was the love of her life."

In the second year, I packed all her things and put them in

cartons in the shed in the back of the house. Someone mentioned at a party that they had seen her working at a government office in Lagos. I pretended to know all about it. Témì was missing her sister, and I didn't know what to do.

"Sweetheart, please tell your daughter to at least talk to her younger sister." I mentioned it to Tító.

"Ládùn has been in touch with her. Témì told me."

"Oh, so I am the only one now?"

"Hassana, stop!"

Témì started to withdraw from me, so I made efforts to go to her. I visited her often in her hostel and cooked her favourite meals. I tried to be more flexible and thought that I knew her. She seemed uncomfortable that I was always in her space.

"If you don't want me to come to your hostel, then come home during the weekend."

"Okay, Màámi. I will come."

"And you can bring Bòbọọ́lá and IK. I know you people are joined at the hip."

Her eyes lit up, and she hugged me. Témì was my own, and I didn't need Ládùn.

The third year, I started to miss my first child. I begged Tító to check on her in Lagos but to pretend I didn't know about his visits.

"Why can't we go together?"

"The girl blames me for all of her life's problems, and she hasn't accepted my friend request on Facebook. I am certain she still hates me."

Tító started to visit her. He would come home and show me

pictures; she looked well. One day, she called me. I was so nervous that I didn't know how to play it after almost three years.

"Yes? Ládùn, how can I help you?" I didn't recognise the sound of my own voice.

I don't remember the rest of the conversation, but she punished us by not speaking to her father for another three months. When they finally started to speak again, he came home and told me, "Ládùn is engaged."

"I don't understand."

"I have not met the guy, but she started dating him last year, and they are engaged."

"Who would want to marry a girl without her parents' permission?"

"Àdùnní stood in for us."

"Ah! Àdùnní is now her family, abi? Who is this man sef?"

"His name is Edache. She told me that it was all very sudden."

"And she wants to marry him?"

"I am tired, Hassana. Let's talk about it tomorrow."

If my children allowed me to plan their lives, all would be perfect. Témì would be a lawyer, married to our neighbour's son, Sọlá, who is an engineer—at least, he will be when he completes his final year of university.

"Sọlá keeps failing EGL 501 because the lecturer hates his father," his mother always mentioned, unprompted, whenever we met at Bible study. "They had a fight during that ASUU meeting, and he has been holding a grudge ever since."

"We will keep praying for him." I like Sọlá. He is a good boy, and no matter how dull he is, he will probably get a job in Canada. They will have beautiful children, and I will visit them.

I would prefer Ládùn to marry an older man who could calmly handle her tantrums. A younger man may actually poison that girl because she has too much anger in her.

LÁDÙN AND LAGOS

Lagos welcomed me with a slap.

"Conductor, please, I am getting off at Ìkejà, under the bridge."
I repeated this twice, so when I found out I was at a place called
Awólówò Way, I refused to get off.

"This na awa las bus stop; you beta get down."

"I told you I was going to stop at Ìkejà, under a bridge."

"Ehn ehn, why you kan sleep forget?"

"I didn't sleep; I dozed off. I also don't know Lagos. I am not
getting off here."

Out of the blue, he dragged me from my seat, shoved me
against the dirty yellow bus, and slapped me. "If you be Johnny
jus come, dis na my welcome-to-Lagos gift!" he barked.

If this was the shade of independence I sought, I would have
splashed a better canvas. Lagos had a loudness about it that I
didn't understand. It was a far cry from Ifè. When I finally alighted
at a petrol station not too far from Àdùnní's house, Àdùnní and
her male friend found me in tears. I was tempted to call home or
at least answer one of my parents' many messages so that my father would come and collect me.

In Lagos, the water was dirty, and horns blared every morning, waking me and Àdùnní up. The power supply was inconsistent, so I sat in the barbershop to charge my phone during the weekends and pretended to be interested in neighbourhood gossip.

"Babe, this is what it means to be an adult. We must be strong. Don't sulk. Just focus," Àdùnní said to me one night.

The apartment we rented in Òpèbí was in a pitiful state. The first time it rained, the ceiling of our bedroom wept.

"Àdùnní, are you sure this roof won't cave in?"

Àdùnní murmured something in her sleep and then snatched the blanket away from me and wrapped it around herself.

"This girl, why do you like doing this? On top of this tiny mattress of ours? Give it to me!"

Àdùnní laughed a little and relaxed her hold on the blanket so we could share again.

The next morning, mud-coloured water rose to the doorstep, and we spent an hour filling buckets and emptying them out through the back door before we could leave.

"Is God angry with Lagos? I don't understand this kind of rain," Àdùnní said as sweat ran down her face. I felt the urge again to call home.

Thankfully, my call-up letter for the National Youth Service Corps came three weeks later. As Àdùnní had promised, we were both posted to Lagos. The city kept me busy that first year. It was traffic-work-traffic-home, repeat the next day. I rested during the weekend so I had enough energy to face the week ahead.

We both got to work in the Civil Service. While Àdùnní was in the Ministry of Finance, I was in Civic Engagement. I would wake up early, get to Aláúsá, Ìkejà, and sleep until eight a.m., when work began. I would clock out at four p.m. and then head back to Òpèbí.

The workplace culture at the Civil Service in Lagos was laid-back. Workers arrived whenever they pleased, spent the day gossiping, pretended to work when queries were sent in, left when they felt like it, then returned the next day to do the same thing. Monday to Friday, I was Ládùn, the Youth Corps member who got food for everyone in the office. The women liked me because I was respectful.

My boss was a hairy middle-aged woman with a wig that was neither Afro nor curls. She wore gold jewellery and would walk around for an hour in the morning, making mundane conversation. "Ahn, Mrs. Jessica, this your blouse is fine *o*. I will eventually use your tailor when her price comes down," she would compliment the head of marketing.

"Hmm, this country, e go better," she would console the accountant who spent every day sharing stories about when things in Nigeria were "good."

"I will be back soon. If any of the Ogas asks for me, ping me on the phone. My house is down the street," she would say, hurrying out.

"Yes, ma."

"Ládùn, just keep your head down, and you will climb up the ladder. You will become a permanent secretary." The secretary always repeated the same advice during lunch break as she wolfed down her usual meal of yam porridge, vegetables, and fish that she brought from home. She was the only one who didn't ask me to get her food.

"I bring my food from home. I don't want anyone to poison me. Civil Service can be brutal, and I still have a long way to go," she would whisper.

I liked her spirit. Even though she was a secretary and typist with only a secondary school certificate, at fifty, she still had dreams of becoming a permanent secretary. "This is the Civil Service; anything can happen."

I told Àdùnní about the secretary's advice.

"Ládùn, please. The Civil Service is for those who are afraid to dream. All they do is gossip, file documents that have no head nor tail, and eat. It is a safe place. We are too young. We will stay if they retain us, but we won't be there for long. We didn't come to Lagos to count bridges."

The men in my office mostly stared at me. The floor manager, Mr. Peter, always made sure to compliment me. "Wow, Ládùn, you are looking good. If I have money, I will take you as my second wife."

"Whenever you are ready," I would play along.

Serving in the Department of Civic Engagement was eye-opening. I saw many weddings, and each had its own feel. One time, a woman came in with a boy who could have been her grandson. She wore a white flared dress, and the groom was dressed in an oversized black suit. The roses she held throughout the ceremony looked as if they had just been plucked from the flowerbed behind the office building.

"It is because she is white. She is his passport to leave this country," the accountant said as we gathered to watch the union from the window.

"So because he wants to leave Nigeria, he is ready to sleep with a person old enough to be his mother?" the secretary responded.

"You never know; the older the berry, the sweeter the juice," Mrs. Jessica remarked, smoothening the ruffles on her blouse.

"That juice don ferment," one of the cleaners chimed in.

The gossip about the old woman and her young husband kept the office alive throughout that week.

Another time, one man came in with three women.

"Please just marry us."

"Sir, we can't do that," I tried to explain to him.

"Ahn ahn, sister, why are you an enemy of progress?" the groom asked.

"You no wan make we marry?" added one of the brides.

On commercial buses, my preference was always the back seat. Àdùnní and I sat close to each other and then used our handbags to ward off unwelcome hands from grazing our breasts and buttocks. One evening after work, we waited for a long time at the bus stop, but there was no bus.

"Na wa o, where are all the buses today sef?" I kicked the stone beside me onto the empty road.

"I am getting tired. I think we should continue hitching rides with my boss," Àdùnní suggested.

"So that he can keep feeling us up like he did the first day he gave us a ride?"

"At least we will not be waiting endlessly."

I also didn't accept free rides because I had read about girls being cut into pieces by strangers. After what seemed like a lifetime of waiting, a black SUV pulled up beside us, and the tinted window rolled down to reveal a young man in traditional garb and a cap.

"Hi, pretty ladies, where are you off to?"

I was about to walk away, but Àdùnní held on to me tightly. "We are going to Òpèbí."

"Ahhh, Òpèbí is not far. Do you girls mind if I give you a ride?" Àdùnní shook her head and bundled me into the back seat while she sat beside him.

A few minutes into the journey, he tried to start a conversation. I was silent, but Àdùnní spoke to him.

"So my name is Paul. I am a club owner, and I have a new club on Allen Avenue. I am looking for two fine young girls who can be my club promoters from Friday to Sunday. I'll pay you twenty thousand naira per weekend, and you'll work for eight hours per day. Your job is just to lure guys into the club; you are both very sexy. Don't worry; I'll assign a bouncer to each of you."

There was that word again—"sexy." Why couldn't men just leave the word alone? Was it a gift? If this man turned out to be a kidnapper, I was sure my mother would be laughing at me. *So, Ládùn, you left the house only to be kidnapped? What a shame!* Àdùnní's voice interrupted my thoughts.

"We can do it for twenty-five thousand each per weekend. You know we have to shop for clothes and pay for transportation."

"You are accepting the job, then?" His eyes met mine in the rearview mirror.

"She will do it!" Àdùnní answered for me.

Paul dropped us off at the junction close to our apartment.

"Àdùnní, so you want us to become prostitutes, abi? You think because my parents are not here, my father's head will not haunt me?"

"Ládùn, together we will make two hundred thousand a month. If we subtract clothes, food, and everything, we can have, like, one hundred thousand left to save."

"Where is Paul going to get that kind of money? What if he is a Yahoo boy?"

"He is not. When you were rushing to get out, he gave me his card."

Àdùnní handed it over to me. I saw that he was also a car dealer. I had seen his dealerships in passing. I really could use the money. If I didn't take the offer, I was most likely going to end up broke, as both my government and the Civil Service allowance did not add up to even twenty-five thousand naira a month.

"Okay, let's do it."

"You won't regret it!" Àdùnní hugged me so tight, it reminded me of Témì. I really should have called her. I just didn't know what to say.

This was how Àdùnní and I both became civil servants by day and club promoters by night.

The first month, I struggled with my new job. The air was stuffy with intermingling odours, and I spent most nights dodging pats on my buttocks, but I knew if I didn't start performing better, I might lose my job. I needed the distraction to keep me from thinking about Mofę and my family. Eventually, I started to enjoy the job, flirted innocently with the men, and sometimes danced more than the club girls who performed private dances. On other nights, I just danced with Àdùnní.

"Ládùn, you will be dancing and seducing the men. Well done *o. Sha* stay within my line of sight so that if anyone tries any nonsense, I can use my teeth to protect you," Àdùnní teased.

There were three types of spenders in the club: the ones who had the money, flaunted, and spent it; the ones who took months before they could clear their tabs; and the ones who didn't have any money but attached themselves to their rich friends to impress young girls. The club was always packed—shiny cars outside and prostitutes lingering around, hoping to catch prey. Those who could afford to buy drinks came into the club and waited until they got their men for the night.

"Ládùn, I just want to fuck you," a regular customer would say while following me around.

"You are not allowed to talk to me like that."

"Do you know how much I spend every weekend on drinks? Come off it. I will talk to you how I like."

Justin, the bouncer who was assigned to me, always ended up stepping in, which seemed to calm the customer down. I could not always avoid customers like this. Part of my job was to encourage them to buy drinks.

"I don't drink," I used to say when I first started, but that only made me lose clients while Àdùnní gained more.

"The trick is to pretend to drink and spit it out when they're not looking. Or just always carry a drink with you. That way, your glass is always full, and no one has to offer you a drink," the club manager advised me. Àdùnní was usually tipsy by the end of the night, but her bouncer kept an eye on her. There was an incident when a customer groped my breasts, and Àdùnní chased him around the club, threatening to bite his balls off. The news spread quickly, and the guys started to avoid touching either of us.

Whenever we had met our quota of a hundred thousand naira spent per night and got our tabs cleared, we feigned tiredness and slid out to the waiting room. Some weekends, I met the quota. Other times, I didn't.

"We must never smoke or do drugs, Ládùn. Remember, this is a bus stop for us; we are going to take over Lagos!" Àdùnní said one afternoon as we counted our tips from the previous night.

There were times when the club became rowdier than usual.

One night, one of the prostitutes rushed into the club, screaming, "Where dat useless guy? For this Lagos, who dey finger me for free? E tink say I be normal person?"

The club manager approached her, and after a couple of minutes, she left with a smile.

"That's the side chick of one of those bank managers. She had a thing with his friend, and he didn't pay her."

"Why did she come in here to shout?"

"The friend is our boss, Ládùn. Better keep quiet and mind your business. They gave her fifty thousand naira, and she left."

I thought Mr. Igwe was different. I had seen him with his wife a couple of times since he employed us. Why would a man with such a beautiful wife sleep with an ashéwó?

Another event that stuck with me was the night the police raided the streets surrounding the club, rounding up all the girls. There was a deafening noise that caused most people to rush out. Àdùnní and I sought cover behind the bar and only came out when the manager found us.

"Ahn ahn, even you, Àdùnní, with your sharp mouth, you still dey run?"

"It is Ládùn I am protecting. Her parents will kill me if anything happens to her."

"You sef, come out now, use your teeth and fight."

"Manager, please let me stay here," I pleaded.

"It is the police jàre. They came to pack away all those ashéwós in front of the club."

"Why?" I asked, after my heart rate had returned to its normal pace.

"That's how they do it. They come suddenly and carry them away. Some pay to get out, but the ones wey never make money go use their toto pay."

"So on top say the babes dey help us by keeping horny men off the streets, police still dey harass them?"

"Na the housewives dey in charge of that law."

Sunday nights, we finished at the club around two a.m. so we could catch some sleep before heading to the office. We would crash in the room the manager gave us at the back of the club, and go to the office from there.

After the year of service to our country was done, Àdùnní and I had each saved up a million naira. "Let's not buy anything. Let's just keep saving," we both agreed. We were both retained in the Civil Service.

The first time my father came to Lagos, I chose to meet him at Shoprite in Ìkejà. It was one of the hottest spots in my neighbourhood. It was always crowded, even on weekdays. I thought it was better to meet him in a crowded place, to avoid uncomfortable conversations.

"Daddy, my apartment is tiny, and I share it with Àdùnní."

"That's okay. I can sit anywhere as long as I spend some time with you. Are you eating and taking care of yourself?"

I half smiled at his attempt to ease the tension hanging over us. "Yes, I am. Thank you, Daddy."

"Do you want to tell me what happened that night with your mother?"

"I don't, sir." I was not ready to talk about the betrayal.

"How is Àdùnní?" He decided to change the subject.

"She is fine."

"Say hello to her from me."

He fished some mint naira notes out of his pocket later as he got into his Corolla.

"Daddyyy," I called out to him like I wanted to object.

"Please don't break my heart any further. It is bad enough that we don't know how you have survived this long. We want to send you money."

"I am fine. I make enough money."

"I don't care. We will send you money going forward. Just help us manage it."

"Thank you, sir."

"Thank your mother too."

"Okay, sir."

"I love you, my first fruit."

"I love you too, Daddy."

I fought tears and the urge to run after him as he drove off. I didn't want him to see the doubt in my eyes, so I waved him off enthusiastically. As I walked to the bus stop, a question nagged at me. If I could see the man my mother said fathered me, what would I say? What can one say to a stranger? A stranger my mother chose to forget. It seemed like the memory really broke my mother. I was not blind to her hurt. I just didn't care.

"So you had a baby and gave it to my daddy."

"I had you, and your father and I are happy."

"So how does Mofẹ́'s father know all this?"

"I told him about the night I slept at Atiku's."

"How did he know you were pregnant?"

"I guess he worked it out from your age or something, because no one except your father and I knows you are not his child."

"Aaahhhhh, Mummy, you are wicked!"

As I looked back, maybe I hadn't responded wisely. But I was dealing with a heartbreak, news of my biological father, and the reality that my whole life was a lie. I knew I was hurting my parents. I just didn't know how to stop being angry.

The second year, Àdùnní met Dr. Sally, who moved us into a two-bedroom flat in Ìkejà GRA. It was a twenty-four-hour service apartment, so our small I-better-pass-my-neighbour generator was able to rest. Her new man was different from the previous ones. Dr. Sally wanted to marry Àdùnní and take her to Dubai. He sent her to do a course at Lagos Business School, so she left the Civil Service. He also invested five hundred thousand naira into my side business when Àdùnní mentioned it to him.

I started selling textiles while working my Civil Service job. Most of my customers were the guys from the club and the ministry, and they also gave me referrals. Within three months, I was supplying local clothing fabrics such as àdìre and Ankara to Lagos designers.

"As my wife's friend, I should encourage you. Girls your age would be looking for sugar daddies otherwise," Dr. Sally said.

I thought it ironic that he made such a statement boldly when he was twice Àdùnní's age, gave her an allowance, and told her to stop working. The Lagos Business School was a distraction to keep her busy while they prepared to leave the country.

"There is nothing in Naija, babe. If no be say you and your parents dey fight and I don't want your mother to curse me, I would have said let's relocate together."

"I won't leave Nigeria like you. Who would rebuild the country if we all did?"

"Ládùn, you can come with me," Àdùnní said with pleading eyes.

"No, thank you. I don't hate my parents *that* much," I said, smiling.

"I don't have parents, so I can't relate, is that it?"

"Nooo . . . that was not—"

"I am just playing," she cut in.

Her man bought her a Nissan CRV.

"Sally says we are relocating next April," she announced excitedly one afternoon as she sauntered into the house.

"Àdùnní, I am happy you have found love, but our agreement was that we would do everything together," I responded.

Àdùnní walked up to me, hugged me, and then whispered into my ear, "Ládùn, please get a boyfriend. Sally sometimes asks me if you have a vendetta against men. He says, 'Every time we go out, men are trying to get her attention, but she will be acting like a possessed woman.'"

Perhaps triggered by Àdùnní's imminent departure, I started being more open to suitors. One quiet evening at the club, Edache came my way. He was six-foot tall, broad-shouldered, with a brawny body that was always clad in T-shirts and jeans. He had a moustache he absentmindedly played with whenever he spoke. Unsurprisingly, the girls on the dance floor all made passes at him. One of the new promoters, Ego, came over to the bar.

"Ládùn, did you see that man that just came in?"

"Ego, go and attend to your tables. Do your work, this girl."

"Abeg, better come and see this fine man. I hope he spends well *o*. If he is single, I will be all his."

The man setting the girls on fire started to frequent the club regularly, and soon became friends with Ego.

"Edache likes you, Ládùn. He has asked me to give you his number."

"Huh?"

"He says you should call him."

Ego sent the number to me, and for a week, I pondered whether to call him. But it soon dawned on me that I was going to be lonely once Àdùnní left. I called him after one Saturday morning cleanup. He picked up on the third ring.

"Hello, this is Edache."

"Hi, this is Ládùn. I am the—"

"Wow! I was hoping you would call."

The conversation was easy. He was twelve years older, had studied at Ahmadu Bello University, did his master's in London, came back to Nigeria, worked at a bank for many years, and now ran a cocktail company.

"So that is enough about me. Tell me about yourself, Ládùn. Can I tell you how beautiful you are? I was scared to talk to you. Please don't hang up," he said, his calm voice soothing my nerves over the phone.

"Thank you. That's very nice of you." The irritation I usually felt when men spoke to me was not there.

Edache continued to frequent the club during the weekends. He was the safest and easiest choice. Within a few weeks, we went from being friends to being in a committed relationship. He recommended my business to his clients. "Baby, I have a wedding I am supplying drinks for. I am trying to get you a contract to do the aso-ebí."

"I don't sell lace, babes."

"You will make plenty of money if you do."

There were so many things I liked about him. He was support-ive of my hustle. He kept me company at the club during the weekends and drove me home. Àdùnní adored him.

"He loves you, Ládùn."

"Na wa! How you know?"

"Ládùn, I want you to marry before Sally and I leave."

"Edache and I have only been together for three months, Àdùnní."

"My dear, you need someone to look after you when I am gone. So please make up with your parents and take him to see them."

"Àdùnní—"

"Ládùn, I am not trying to tell you how to treat your parents. We all have parental baggage; I just don't want you to be alone."

The following week, Edache brought up marriage while we were shopping for lace. It was for a client whom he had secured for me.

"This girl, you don't pay me commission because I am your man."

"I pay you with pecks and hugs."

"I want the real thing," he said as he raised his eyebrows play-fully. "On a serious note, I want us to discuss the possibility of you and me getting married."

"You are asking me about marriage when we are in Balogun Market, sweating like this?"

"Ládùn, even with your sweat, you are more ravishingly beau-tiful than any babe here. But no problem, I'll ask you again."

That was exactly what he started to do; he asked every week. "I will keep asking you to marry me until you say yes."

"It is too soon."

When I saw my dad that month, I wanted to tell him about Edache's proposals, but he was more interested in the rift with my mother.

"Ládùn, I know we agreed we wouldn't talk about it, but please, how long will you stay angry at your mother? Besides, we both lied to you; it wasn't just your mother."

"No, you fell in love with her, and she roped you into her lies."

"My first fruit, you can't be that naïve. I did it because you are my child, and I never want to see you hurt. You are my child, Ládùn."

"Daddy, I lost Mofẹ́ because of Mummy's lies."

"No, you lost Mofẹ́ because he wasn't man enough to fight for you. What kind of man fights his father's fight? Are you your mother? Why pay for her sins? You dodged a bullet with Mofẹ́, and you will realise that with time. Stop punishing your mother for something she didn't mean to do."

"I can't talk about it now. Lagos is crazy."

"I brought you some vegetables." He put a plastic bag in my hands. "I also have a picture of your birth father and his name with me. Your mother and I saved it for you. If you ever want to look for your father—"

"Daddy, not now." I moved close to hug him, and his familiar aftershave enveloped me. "You are my father, and I am your daughter."

"Then come home. Three years is a long time to punish your parents."

"Daddy, let's not talk about it."

"You are as stubborn as your aunty Jummai." He gave me the things and left.

I had forgotten to bring up Edache.

TÉMÌ'S SILENCE

When Ládùn left home, you felt invisible. You missed your sister. But still you knew you were not alone. You had family—broken, restless, stubborn, imperfect. But they were still family. The morning of the day she left, a plate had smashed on the kitchen floor. It was an omen. That night, after leaving Bòbóọlá's house, you got to the entrance of your home and heard distant voices from the living room, your mother's the loudest. Your sister screamed back, and you heard her screams turn into sniffles. "I am not coming back here," she threatened.

You walked into the scene, deafened by the harsh words that were flying like darts between your loved ones. No one saw you. You reached out and touched your sister's skirt. "Ládùn . . ." She flinched and slapped your hand away. You watched her drag her luggage into Àdùnní's car.

"Màámi?" You walked toward your mother.

"Not now, Témì. Go and sleep, please!" She walked away.

Aunty Jummai was muttering words you couldn't make out.

You went into your room, but you didn't sleep. No one slept that night.

Ládùn's absence was felt everywhere, and you didn't under-

stand why no one seemed to acknowledge it, not even Aunty Jummai. It was as if Ládùn had died, and you'd missed the funeral.

You missed everything about her, but the one thing you
craved the most was the peace you felt when you were both lying
on her bed, together in comfortable silence. One such evening
came to mind.

"I love how calm we both are even when we have nothing to
say to each other. I'd choose this any day over conversation with
my classmates."

"Ládùn, your words are sweet. You should think about being a
writer!"

"We are Yoruba, Témì. Words are our superpower. You have it
too; that's why you always get into trouble with Big Mummy and
Aunty Jummai."

"But I don't say anything."

"Silence is powerful, especially when the person you are spar-
ring with is screaming."

"Témì, come and board at the hostel. It will help you to stop
thinking about Ládùn so much," IK suggested after you told him
and Bòbọọlá about the night she left.

"See, I understand Màámi acting up. It's my dad I don't get. He
is also being weird. I have called Ládùn several times, texted
her . . . but no response."

"We have all called her. She is not picking up. If your parents
aren't worried, you shouldn't be too. Just pray for her," Bòbọọlá said.

"Come to the hostel," IK cajoled.

"Okay."

That evening, you asked for their permission. You moved to the hostel, and shortly after, your mother started visiting every weekend.

"Just because you are in the hostel doesn't mean you are an adult; you are still my baby," she would say.

"Màámi, please call me first. I don't want my roommate to think I am a mummy's girl."

"Okay, my big girl. I will."

Then she would visit again without calling. So you just let her have her way.

Bòbóólá and IK became your rocks. Bòbóólá also became the poster girl for snatching other girls' boyfriends. She was popular from the first semester.

"Bobby, can't you just find a single guy?" you asked.

"The guys I date are single. Last time I checked, they weren't wearing a ring."

"One of their other girlfriends will eventually find you and beat you."

As you predicted, karma soon caught up with her. Unfortunately, the day it did, you were at her side. You had just finished your lecture at the amphitheatre, and Bòbóólá called, offering to pick you up in her new boo's car.

"I can find my way, Bobby."

"No, I insist. I will pick you up. The guy drives a G-Wagon. You are my bestie, so I will spoil you silly."

"You know my parents work on this campus, right? So I can't be seen in a car they didn't buy for me."

"Don't worry; the windows are tinted."

You had hung up and were contemplating taking a bus when she showed up in a bright blue car with the promised tinted windows. The speakers were blasting Wizkid's "Ojúelégba" as the car pulled over, and Bòbóọlá rolled down the windows.

"Hey, sexy mama. Going somewhere? Gosh! Témì, you are so pretty."

"Lies . . . but thank you. At least if man won't *toast* me, my best friend is permitted to lie to me."

"No lie. Your face is stunning."

"Na my face we go chop?"

"Hop in, baby. We are going to town."

"I hope Daddy's friend doesn't report me. I think I saw his Afro around the corner, buying meat pie," you said, getting into the car.

"You are a good child. They will be fine. *My* parents won't be surprised. My mother knows I am a mad person."

She was about to drive off when a red Corolla screeched to a halt beside the driver's door, effectively blocking traffic. Bòbóọlá swore.

You jumped out of the car. "Hey! What do you think you are—"

Slap.

You staggered back onto the pavement, but a stranger's hand steadied you.

Bòbóọlá scrambled out through the passenger side. "Are you mad? Why did you slap her?"

Slap.

The rage on the young woman's face belied her slight frame. "So you are the that is sleeping with my fiancé."

A small crowd had started to gather, phones raised, recording the spectacle. You knew it was going to be in the gossip blogs, so you pulled Bọ̀bọọ́lá close. The blogs had a field day whenever Bọ̀bọọ́lá was in the news. She was clickbait.

The moment Bọ̀bọọ́lá felt you pulling at her, she started struggling.

"Leave her, Bọ̀bọọ́lá," you pleaded.

"No! Why did she slap my friend? Let me just finish this psycho." Bọ̀bọọ́lá folded her hands into fists and took on a fighting stance. "I will beat you, ehn!"

The stranger ran to her car and came back immediately, brandishing a knife. The crowd shrank back, keeping a safe distance.

"Come now, let me stab you. I will kill you, kill her, and then kill myself!"

"Kill who?" Bọ̀bọọ́lá started to take off her slippers.

You pulled her arm hard and whispered in her ear, "If you struggle too much, I will leave you, and we both know you don't know how to fight. Are you ready to die?"

People from the crowd held the aggrieved woman back, and you and Bọ̀bọọ́lá made a quick escape, getting back into the car through the passenger side and locking all doors as Bọ̀bọọ́lá zoomed off.

A few minutes into the drive, you broke the silence. "See how that babe used slap to rearrange my face? All because I was sitting in her fiancé's G-Wagon!"

"I am sorry. It's not even about the car."

"Bọbọ́lá, return the car and leave the guy alone."

"The owner of this car is not her fiancé. That babe is the girl-friend of my other man. Can you imagine? Someone I am planning to break up with. I hope she didn't scratch your beautiful face, Témì? You should have let me beat her up."

You looked at her, your mouth slightly ajar. "You want to fight a woman holding a knife? You are crazy!"

"That makes two of us, baby!" She chuckled. You laughed too. All was forgotten.

One day, during your second semester, IK's elder brother, Chuka, a medical student, came to visit him. IK brought him to your room in Moremi B204.

"You didn't tell me you were bringing a very important visitor."

"Chuka, meet my best friend, Témì. Témì, my elder brother—even though he is only older by a year."

"Nice to meet you." You pretended not to stare. Where IK was handsome, Chuka was perfection. His coily hair reached down almost to his eyebrows, and his sideburns connected to his beard. His fair skin was shiny, as if it had been polished.

"Can I offer you some jollof rice?"

Your roommate, Dorothy, had just made rice, and she enjoyed sharing her food. She was a Jehovah's Witness, and she never hid her desire to have you join them. "Témì, just come with me to one of our meetings."

"Dorothy, I am not even sure I like God, let alone like him well enough to become a Jehovah's Witness."

"Don't worry; God loves you enough to wait until you fall for him."

"Please leave me be."

She was a good person and a fantastic cook.

"Thank you, but Ikenna and I already made dinner plans," Chuka said, quietly interrupting the chaos in your head. His voice was not too deep, but it was clear it belonged to a man. "Témì, I have heard so much about you."

"Good things, I hope?"

"Yes. Ikenna eats, drinks, and lives for Témì. I can see why." He held your gaze, and after a few seconds, you broke eye contact.

Was he talking about your skinny frame? Did he think his brother pitied you because you were thin and had no buttocks? You felt your crush slip away. You came up with an excuse and didn't join them for dinner despite IK and Chuka begging you. After that, you avoided Chuka. He came to Ilé-Ifẹ̀ a few more times, but you always found an excuse not to see him. You weren't quite sure why Chuka took such an interest in you. IK would mention in passing, "Chuka asked after you."

"My regards to him," you would respond.

You didn't want him laughing at you or telling his brother he could get better-looking friends. Out of sight, out of mind.

Ládùn reached out in your second year of university. She replied to your message on Facebook. No one was willing to explain what had happened, and even Ládùn started talking to you as if she hadn't been absent for nearly two years. It was bizarre.

"Ládùn, I sent you several messages."

"No vex, I was really busy. I have missed you, àbúrò."

"I have missed you too."

"What has been happening?"

How did she expect you to summarise two years? Did she want you to tell her how you had heard your mother crying silently on many nights? Or how your father was a shadow of himself since his favourite child left? Or how you had to rely on IK and Bòbọ́lá so you wouldn't become an emotional wreck?

"Nothing really. You haven't missed much."

"This is my new number. You can call me anytime. Love you, sis."

The person on the other end of the line was Ládùn, but you knew your sister was a different person. Still, you were grateful that she had made contact—that was enough for you.

LÁDÙN AND EDACHE

At the beginning of my third year in exile, I decided to go home, settle things with my parents, and then marry Edache. I called my father to give him the news, but he didn't pick up. So I finally called my mum, who answered on the third ring.

"Yes?"

"Good afternoon, ma."

"Ládùn, what do you want? Why not call your father, please?" Her voice was sharp. How dare this woman sound that way after everything she put me through with her lies? I hung up, fury coursing through me as I dialled Edache.

"Hi, baby," he answered.

"Do you still want to marry me?"

"Every day."

"Then let's do it."

"Yes!"

I called Àdùnní immediately after and broke the news. Her silence was not what I expected.

"Hello, is anybody there?" I said after a minute.

"Congratulations, but I don't think you should marry him until you get things sorted with your parents. Ládùn, I know I told you to find someone, but marriage is serious. It is bad enough that your parents think I took you away."

"I don't need their consent."

"Yes, you do."

She was right, so I told Edache to hold on. The next day, when he walked through the club doors, I ran to him. "Babe, we are engaged, and I promise you that I will marry you, but let us hold on a little longer."

"What happened? You were ready yesterday." Edache's confusion was etched on his brow.

"I am ready today, but I need to work things out with my parents before we take the leap."

"You are trying to avoid sex, abi? I don't mind waiting, Ládùn. I have not pressured you, have I?"

"Just give me time," I pleaded with him.

"Okay, my wife-to-be."

My father called me for three months, but I didn't pick up his calls. It was only on his birthday that I spoke with him.

"Happy birthday, Daddy."

"My first fruit, you finally decided to return my calls. Happy birthday in advance to you too! This phone call has made my day."

"Thank you. Since I moved to Lagos, I haven't been celebrating my birthday."

"I miss our joint celebrations."

"Titó, come and cut your cake! Who is that?" I heard my mother's voice in the background.

"Ládùn," he responded.

"Daddy, I will call you another time. Love you." I ended the call quickly before I was forced to speak to my mother.

Four months later, while we were sitting in a restaurant opposite the Shoprite mall in Ìkejà, I told him that I had gotten engaged.

"Ládùn, you called me, but I couldn't answer. You called your mother, she was a bit on the edge, and you decided to get engaged?"

"I am sorry, Daddy."

"This man asked you to marry him without your parents' consent? Did you tell him we were dead?"

"No, sir."

"What kind of man wants to marry you without knowing your people? Marriage is about families."

"He is an orphan."

"So he thinks you fell from the sky?"

After a short pause, he continued, "You know if you want to see your biological father, you have our permission. Maybe that will give you some peace."

Silence.

"Let me be going, Ládùn. I'll see you next month." As he stood to leave our usual meeting spot, he stopped in his tracks and said, "Anger at your parents is understandable. But this thing you have done is an insult. I really thought I meant more to you."

I cried that night and told Edache about my father's concerns.

"Let's go and see them tomorrow," he suggested.

"No, my father has asked me to give him some time."

Àdùnní left in October of 2019 for Dubai. I started to spend more time with Ego, who had quit working as a club promoter to get married.

"Ládùn, I know you miss Àdùnní, but please try to have a good time at my wedding."

"How much is the aso-ebí?"

"This girl, with all your hustle and your fiancé's money, you are still worried about the price?"

"My dear, this is Nigeria; one dollar is now almost four hundred naira."

After the wedding, I called my father to apologise. When I sensed his relief that he was back on speaking terms with me, I said, "Daddy, Edache wants to come and see you."

"Ládùn, you need to settle things with your mother first."

"Daddy, he can meet you somewhere."

"Does he intend to come and ask for your hand in a restaurant? Ládùn, make up with your mother. Then he can come see us both. How well do you even know this man?"

"I already know him. We have been together for almost a year."

"Okay, give it another year then."

"Daddy, it sounds like you are saying it is too early."

"No. I met and married your mother within a month."

"Exactly!"

"But you are not us. Your generation is always in a hurry. Your mother and I married because I wanted to shut people up before they asked questions about you."

"So she basically used you."

"Ládùn, for the last time, I chose to marry your mother knowing that she was pregnant. I chose to be with her. I *begged* her. Please stop with this constant blame game. You are making too many decisions from a place of hurt. I have never felt more at peace than when your mother and I chose each other."

I was not ready for his truths. Covid came soon after, and I moved in with Edache.

Living with Edache was the same as being married, but still I decided not to rush anything. I didn't see my dad for another six months because interstate travelling was prohibited. During that time, I fell in love with Edache even more.

"I don't want to rush you into having sex, but since Covid has put our lives on hold, let's start making babies," he said one evening in April.

"My parents won't like that."

"Babe, we are going to get married anyway, so what's the big deal?"

"I appreciate your patience, but—"

Edache interrupted, "Let's not forget that you are not a virgin. Your ex already popped that cherry."

"Really?"

"Nobody knows when this pandemic will end. I am not saying this because I want us to have sex. If I can restrain myself while living in the same house with you and this body of yours, I can overcome any temptation. I just want a baby." Over the coming weeks he kept talking about us becoming parents.

"I will think about it." How could I tell the man I was engaged to that I could still feel Mofẹ́ between my legs when I dreamt about him? How could I explain that a part of me was still tied to Mofẹ́?

Eventually, Edache wore me down. My first night with him was in May 2020.

"Thank God *o*. I am finally sleeping with my woman."

I didn't mention to him that I also started birth control that night.

Sometime in June, I logged into my Facebook account, and there it was, a message from Mofẹ́:

Hi Ládùn,

I know you hate me.

I am so sorry, but my father told me that he would kill himself if I ever spoke to you or about you. Family first.

I know you have found someone. I hope he makes you happy because you deserve it. I am sorry.

My family is everything to me.

Hopefully we can be friends someday.

Friends? The fucker wanted to be friends? Something broke in me. That night, I stopped taking my birth control pills and decided Edache could fuck me pregnant so I could forget about Mofẹ́. As soon as Edache came home from the estate football game, I pinned him against the wall by the entrance.

"Babe, wait . . . wait . . . let me shower."

"No need."

"I am sweating."

I put my teeth on his earlobe, biting softly. "I like you sweaty."

His eyes closed immediately. I started kissing him while I busied my hands with his shorts, putting my hands into his boxers. He was already hard and warm. Without taking his lips away from mine, he fought his way out of his shorts and sneakers. We walked backward to the nearest sofa, and he flipped me over.

"I am going to get you pregnant tonight."

"Promise?"

"Ládùn, I will put my son in you!"

He slid into me from behind, holding on to my hair, and we went at it for ten glorious minutes. I knew because I was facing the clock that hung in the living room, and I kept seeing Mofẹ́'s face on the clock. Edache didn't get me pregnant that night, but he fucked Mofẹ́ out of my mind. For good.

Later that night, as Edache snored softly beside me, the conversation I'd had with my dad nagged at me, so I decided to look my biological father up. He was now living in America with his family. I kept looking at his face; I didn't look anything like that man. I had my mother's face and my dad's spirit. Why hadn't my mother told me about him? What if I had run into him accidentally? What if I had even spoken with him?

The weeks after Mofẹ́'s message passed quickly. Edache began to fret over my still-flat belly.

"I don't understand. We are both young and healthy. Why is there no baby? Let us go and see your parents. Perhaps it is their prayers that are holding us back."

"I will go first, and then we can go together after. Don't worry. We will get pregnant soon," I reassured him.

"We have to. Otherwise, we need to start IVF."

I hoped for a baby to come naturally, because I had heard from Àdùnní that assisted conception was emotional torture.

"Babes, Dr. Sally has low sperm motility, and I have what they call an inhospitable womb. Just imagine!"

"Huh?"

"His sperm are slow, and even when they get to the uterus, the uterus tries to kill them!"

"I am sorry, Àdùnní," I said quietly.

"My sister, there is nothing I can do."

"You can come back to Nigeria."

"To do what? I would rather put up with my husband than come back. You and Edache should come too. Nigeria is not looking good, babes. Everyone is leaving."

"Àdùnní, please stop with this 'leave Naija' propaganda."

When the #EndSARS movement broke out in October, it took the baby pressure off me for a while. Nigerians had tired of the police force. The police had killed enough people that families feared for their loved ones every day when they stepped out.

"I hate the police. I hope this movement succeeds. My love, we are participating in this protest. In fact, I will supply drinks to people in Aláúsá," Edache said to me. That was how we became involved in the protest. One day, Edache left one of his phones at home and called me. "Babe, please, I left my other phone on the bathroom counter. Can you please put it in the bedside drawer?"

"Okay."

As I went to get the phone, it beeped, and I saw a message.

Meeting for the Covid-19 relief camps raid tomorrow at 8 p.m. Boss, it will be nice for you to come and ginger the guys.

I tapped the screen and gasped. The thread revealed that Edache was the mastermind behind the recent bank robberies in Ìkòròdú. He hadn't carried the guns—Edache was too smooth for that—but he was the head of operations. I skimmed through the flurry of messages.

Boss, the operation was successful. We are doing research on that area that we discussed. Na only food dey the warehouse sha so we can take it and resell.

Idom, the contact who had sent the text, sent another while I was reading.

Help me greet our small madam, boss.

If I hadn't been in shock, I might have laughed. So armed robbers too had a head of operations. As I sat in my car later, trying to process the reality of being an armed robber's fiancée and possible ally, my thoughts were all over the place. Edache, an armed robber? A thief? I had been trying to get pregnant by a thief?

I confronted him when we came home after the protest.

"Edache, I saw a message on your phone."

"Oh yeah? Why were you going through my phone?" He kept eating, but I noticed he chewed more slowly.

"I saw your messages, Edache. Are you an armed robber?"

His face suddenly became hard. His eyes looked void of emotion, and he flexed his jaw as he pushed his plate away. I followed him as he stormed off into the living room. In that moment, his house, in all its three-thousand-square-feet glory, felt very small. He sat down and spoke slowly. "Honestly, how do you think we have survived in this pandemic? How many people are buying textiles or going clubbing? I bought you a car. Come on, Ládùn, don't be so naïve. Surely you didn't think all this comfort came from the proceeds of event-planning?"

He saw me struggling for words, so he went on. "Besides, the things we steal are stolen from the people by the government, and we return them to the people at a small price. I like to think I am stealing from the rich and giving to the poor."

I folded my arms across my chest. "So you are the Ìkejà Robin Hood."

His eyes bulged as if I had just punched him. "If you had stayed at home to receive proper training from your parents, you wouldn't be talking to your husband-to-be like that. Ládùn, please, I am not in the mood to fight."

"I just want a yes or no."

"I am not an armed robber. I am educated, and I don't carry guns. I have people for that. Do you see me complaining about your mediocre cooking? This is what happens when you leave your parents' house before they finish training you. Hell, you don't even know how to suck a dick properly! My dear, we both have our shortcomings, so let's just move on."

My vision became blurry and my palms sweaty. The ground shifted beneath my feet, and I fainted. When I woke up, Edache was beside me in the hospital. He took my hand, and he told me that being a "big boy" wasn't easy. His event-planning business was a front for the organisation. His main source of income was taking hard-earned money from banks and investing it in himself.

The next day, before Edache stopped by to check on me, the doctor broke the news.

"Please don't tell my partner that I am pregnant. I would like to tell him myself."

"But he is your husband, he—"

"Doctor, that man is not my husband yet. Please let me tell him when I am better."

Edache had offered to pick me up from the hospital but I told him to give me time to think. What do you do with the baby a thief put inside you? What do you do when you have intentions of leaving your man, who is an armed robber? These thoughts kept running in my head as I sat in an Uber on my way home. Leaving was not an option yet, so I told Edache that I had forgiven him and would keep his secret safe.

Over the weeks that followed, Edache's eyes followed me everywhere I went. I spent many nights planning my departure. I devised a plan to make him less suspicious.

"Sweetheart, I think we should try doing a detox," I suggested one evening while we were both at home.

"Why?"

"So we can get pregnant."

I could see he was relieved, and he stopped watching me so intently. I didn't have a plan, but I was not going to marry an armed robber or have his baby. It made sense then why he only drove cars with tinted windows, and why he didn't have any social media accounts. It also became clear why he never had a bank card. There was a time I had walked in on him while he was having a meeting with his business partners. There were three Ghana-Must-Go bags of cash beside the three-seater sofa.

"Babe, you came back early. This is good. I wanted to surprise you with a shopping spree. Please take some cash from the drawer on the left-hand side and do some damage at that boutique you like."

I squealed. "Seriously?"

"Yes, my baby love."

"Please introduce me to your friends."

"These are not my friends, babe. You are the only friend I have. They are wedding planners."

Sitting in my shop one evening after Edache's revelation, I remembered a story my father had told me. I wondered if I could go home, like the prodigal son. A month later, I booked an appointment at a clinic I had found online to have the pregnancy terminated. I planned to go home to my family, so we could start over.

As soon as my mind was set, I got the call from Témì that my daddy had died. I was howling out of deep regret, and the doctor assumed it was because I had just killed the baby Edache put in me.

I cried until the doctor had someone escort me to my car.

I had never felt such pain before, not even on the day I left everything behind. The pain was bitter, and it made my tongue swell. Later that night, after I had packed a small bag, Edache came home from work.

"I am going home tomorrow," I said as he lay beside me.

"Is there a problem?"

"No. I just need to see my sister. I will be back within a week."

"Is it not time I met them? I hope they don't think it's my fault. This is on you, my love. I am tired." He yawn-kissed me.

"Yes, of course it is on me. We will pick a date for a meeting this weekend. I won't need the driver, though. Ifè is not Lagos. Life is safer there." I was grateful he didn't slide his hand down my thigh or prolong the kiss.

"I will miss you," he said against my lips. I gripped the sheets and only loosened my hold when he relaxed against the pillow by his side of the bed.

"Me too. Good night."

I texted Ego as Edache snored gently beside me.

Babes, I need a car and a driver for a week. I am travelling to Ilé-Ifè.

Ego responded three hours later. Urgency meant nothing to her. If I needed her badly, I had to go to her house. I was still awake when the text came in, because grief had taken sleep from me too.

Hi boo. Sure. His name is Sylvester.

He is a very good driver +23481302019744

TÉMÌ

In the second semester of your third year, three of your course mates returned with bigger breasts and big buttocks. They were popular members of the Deeper Life Fellowship Church who shared pamphlets during lectures. So when they showed up with their new looks, the university blogs and newspapers ran their stories for months. They didn't seem to care.

"Wow! Do you see those Deeper Life babes? They have really glowed up," you said to Bòbọọ́lá.

"Glowed up under the knife in Nigeria." Bòbọọ́lá's voice was laced with boredom.

"Knife?" you asked. You were sure Bòbọọ́lá was exaggerating again.

"All the Nigerian celebrities are doing it. There are many doctors now in the business of panel-beating women's bodies."

At the end of your third year, you went viral. Bòbọọ́lá's fight with the crazy fiancée resurfaced, and people chose to focus on the flat ass in the video.

"Who is that one with no bumbum?"

"Ahan ahn, why will someone use that girl as a backdrop?"

"Omo, bumbum is scarce."

You didn't know about the video until Dorothy showed you, and you quickly realised it was your backside they were talking about. You were only in it for a minute, but your ass was all anyone talked about. Luckily, the clip didn't show your face. You trashed the outfit you had worn that day and walked around campus hoping no one would recognize your butt, which had become infamous.

It was around that time you first saw the Instagram Reel featuring Sylvia the Influencer, whose life had changed for the better when she went down the cosmetic surgery route. You also saw a clique of girls in your department who went under the knife and suddenly became lecturers' favourites and the "it girls" on campus.

At the start of your final year, your friendships were solid and your grades were good. You and Ládùn were in touch, although it was mostly via text. The messages were surface-level, as if you were both afraid of digging deep, but at least you knew she was only a call away.

Then everything changed.

It was the year that the ASUU embarked on another strike and Covid came in full force to Nigeria.

On the day the school announced that students had to vacate the hostels, you were all at a cybercafe in Old Buka Market, waiting for IK. He'd dragged you there to make copies of a last-minute assignment given by his lecturer.

"Just imagine!" Ikenna said. "This wicked man is giving us pandemic assignments, and this is even an elective course."

"Thank God I didn't pick that course. I am going home to sleep." Bòbọọ́lá laughed at IK's predicament.

IK glared at Bòbọọ́lá. "By the way, I am not leaving the hostel. I don't want to go home. My parents don't like it when I show up and stay for too long. So I'll just be alternating between your crib and Bobby's as well."

"Please, who is going to feed you at mine? You know my dad hates men being around me. Squat at Témì's house, not mine," Bòbọọ́lá responded.

"With friends like Bòbọọ́lá, who needs enemies?" IK retorted.

You watched them bicker for a while before interrupting. "I love how you guys indirectly express love to each other. I think we should attend online tutorials, and maybe build a social media account as 'the three musketeers.' We can make some money off YouTube."

"Témì, YouTube doesn't pay well. I have told you," Bòbọọ́lá said.

"Aunty, let her talk. Not all of us have capital thanks to plenty of men flocking around us," IK smirked.

"We'll do what we can until the strike and pandemic end. I am sure they will be over in a couple of weeks."

Three months into the school strike, Covid had become the hottest topic for discussion in many homes in Ilé-Ifẹ̀'s staff quarters. While some believed it to be a myth, others thought it was real but sought traditional solutions to the virus.

"Just use salt and water to bathe every morning," said a doctor on Instagram who had capitalised on the virus to garner views. A popular pastor assured viewers that there was no Covid and the devil was just trying to distract them. "Drink garlic, ginger, and lemon every morning," he posted on TikTok.

ASUU called off its strike, but students couldn't return to universities while the virus persisted, so you were home alone. IK's parents had asked him to return home before he got caught up by the curfew that had just been declared in most states. So it was just you and Bobby.

You had a fixed routine. You stayed at home in the morning, visited Bòbọọ́lá in the evening before curfew, and chatted with IK on the phone at night, whenever he was available. He always seemed to be tied up.

IK complained to you every evening. "Témì, I am my parents' errand-and-wash boy. Chuka is always studying and doesn't have time for me. This virus needs to go away."

"It will soon be over. Also, Bòbọọ́lá says hello."

"Do you know she has not called me once? I sent her a message, but she ignored me."

"Everyone is trying to cope with the pandemic."

"That girl is just badly behaved."

"Ikenna, you and Bòbọọ́lá are going to be in each other's lives forever because of me, so please learn to put up with her. She is not as bad as you think."

The Bòbọọ́lá you had come to know and love started disappearing about three months into the pandemic. You sent her many messages, but she ghosted you.

Bobby, where did you go?
I am bored. Is this how I am going to spend the pandemic, at
home by myself?
You and Ikenna are wicked sha. That one went to the east, and
you have disappeared.
Hey, I stopped by your house.

After two weeks, she responded.

Fine girl, my dad asked me to do something for him impromptu.
I'll be back in two weeks.

Témì responded,

Ahn ahn, at least pick up calls and answer texts. I miss you.
Sorrryyy.

After speaking on the phone, she ghosted you again. You persisted in texting her for four more weeks without getting a response. Then you let her be. But you kept wondering what the reason for the sudden change could be. You decided to visit her again.

"My dear, you know your friend. She is restless, and this Covid-19 has fuelled her impatience. She can't sit still for a week, even now," her mum explained.

"Please, ma, does she have another number?"

"Témì, she doesn't even answer my texts or calls. There's no way I can find out if she has another number." Bòbóólá's mother's lips quivered as she spoke about Bobby, so you decided not to bother her parents again.

TikTok, Instagram, and Twitter were your go-to distractions. You spent hours on the apps. Bòbọ́lá was still not taking your calls, but you saw her posting content every other day. There were videos of her trying new outfits and singing along to newly released songs with the camera focused on her lips. You left comments on each video, but she ignored them.

As you began your research on going under the knife like you and Bòbọ́lá had discussed, the universe sent you a confirmation in the form of a viral TikTok video. In it, both male and female participants were asked which body part was most attractive to them.

Eighty percent said bumbum. "Breast will come when she gets pregnant. I choose bumbum."

Lectures resumed online, but the site kept crashing, so the university asked all final-year students to return while the other students stayed at home. You had planned to stay in the same hostel as Bobby for your final year, but since you couldn't even contact her to firm up the plans, you ended up staying at Moremi Hall, hoping that she would opt for Moremi too. Her father had been appointed as the new vice chancellor.

You decided to do your thesis on cosmetic surgery, and tried to find clever ways of weaving it into your analysis of the English language.

"Témì, I don't understand this choice of subject. What does this have to do with the use of modern slang?" your supervisor, Dr. Ousane, asked, his scepticism plain to see.

"I am focusing on body dysmorphia, sir, especially in the university system."

"'Bumbum: The African Woman's Language in Modern Nigeria' doesn't seem relevant."

"This is 2020, sir. Everyone's thinking has either evolved or become damaged, plus in my class alone, I know more than ten girls who have undergone cosmetic surgery in order to augment their buttocks."

"This is very interesting. Okay, if you can make a strong argument with your first chapter and proposal, then you may go ahead."

"Thank you, sir."

You came up with a plan. You conducted surveys and recorded voice interviews with the small number of students on campus.

"Yes, the moment I changed my body, my life changed."

"My bumbum has paid my bills, and I already have a job waiting for me because the manager fell in love with my figure despite the fact that she is a woman!"

"My bumbum is natural sha, but the moment I give birth, I am going under the knife."

"I wear a waist trainer to sleep, and I wake up in it. I can't afford surgery yet, but I will do it soon."

"I wear fake hips and bumbum. Once it is time for me and my boyfriend to knack, I off light."

"Of course, I am saving for my labour market makeover—new breast, new butt, and eventually a new nose. I don't like the bridge of my nose."

After two weeks of field research, you showed your supervisor your first chapter.

"This won't work, Témì," he said.

"Okay, sir. I'll change the topic to something more language-based."

"Thank you. Greet your parents for me."

Your supervisor didn't approve the topic, but you at least had enough information for your possible surgery.

During all this, you tried to reach out again to Bọ̀bọọ́lá. You went back to her house, and her mother told you that she had moved to town. Town was where the big girls lived.

You remembered when the story broke about rich men visiting girls in their flats in town, taking them on boat cruises, and then the girls mysteriously disappearing. Bọ̀bọọ́lá was especially wary of the online blogs. "I can't stay in town. God forbids it. The blogs will crucify me," she'd said in your second year. Now she was staying in the same town she had once feared.

At the end of the first semester of your final year, you were on your way back to the staff quarters, listening to music through your earphones—Adékúnlé Gold was asking his God to pick up his phone call so he could be as rich as Dangote. Out of nowhere, a red RAV4 nearly ran you over at a junction. The driver parked quickly.

"I am so sorry. Did I hit you?" A very curvy person ran toward you. She looked familiar.

"No—Bọ̀bọọ́lá?"

"Témì?" She hugged you briefly, then awkwardly withdrew when she felt you draw back.

"Wow, so I can actually run into you on this campus."

"Don't say that *now*. I have been busy."

"Too busy to return my calls or texts? I am your sister, Bobby."

"I am sorry. Get in. We can talk, and I'll drop you off."

She told you she'd lost her phone and contacts. She took you to her new place. It was a two-bedroom flat.

"I met someone, Témì. He is a politician who has three wives, but he loves me. He even paid for my new body. Well, he kind of paid. You like it?"

"What do you mean 'kind of'? Do you owe money to the surgeon? You look like a pineapple, Bọ̀bọọ́lá. The yansh no balance." You wanted to hurt her with the truth.

Her face fell as she tentatively lowered herself onto the sofa beside you. "Témì, are you serious? I took out a loan to do a Brazilian butt lift. It is the money my man gives me that I am using to pay it back. I am almost done with the repayments."

"I thought we agreed to do this together. Look at your ass. I didn't recognise you."

"Yes, but Dubai Papi—that's my man's nickname—loves my body. I did it in Mexico." She said it in a way that inferred that she didn't stoop to having it done by Nigerian doctors.

"Bobby! Mexico? Isn't that the worst place for the procedure? No wonder you look like you're carrying a load of cement."

"Do you know how many followers I have online because of this body? I am international, babes."

"A Nigerian doctor would have beaten you into shape. Because this is panel-beating that was done for you, like on a car, not surgery. I am not even going to get into the Dubai-daddy gist, because I saw that online. You're so beautiful. Why would you choose a man of fifty-five? Then you took a loan to do BBL? It doesn't make sense!"

"These young boys just fuck me and break my heart. I need someone with money, who values me."

"The way you play all of them? How do you want them to take you seriously?"

"That is not nice, Témì."

"I am sorry. What I mean is, we will leave school and meet serious men. Life is just starting for us. You can even redo your body when I get my own done."

Bọbọọlá went quiet, and you felt the change in the room. She dropped you off with mumbled promises to keep in touch. Somehow, that ended the friendship.

Within a few months, all you had was yourself, Ikenna, and Ládùn when she could respond. With Aunty Jummai's help, you began selling hair extensions, and you put all your energy into it. Your business boomed because you knew what the students wanted. They loved that the hair you sold was good quality, yet affordable. You soon doubled your capital.

When the second semester break came, Ikenna went home, but you continued to speak regularly.

"Ehn ehn, Témì, Chuka asked for your number. Should I give it to him?"

"Which Chuka?"

"How many Chukas do you know, this girl? My brother."

"Please don't give it to him."

"I knew you would say no. My brother is a good guy, sha. And he is very popular with the ladies."

"My point exactly. Guys like your brother only like fine, hot babes."

"Fine, hot babes like you. Speaking of fine, hot babes, I met this girl on TikTok. She is an influencer but it turns out she also studies law at a private university. She lives in Aba, so we are meeting soon. I like her."

If you were that fine, why didn't Ikenna ever make passes at you? What exactly was his brother's problem? If Chuka came between you and Ikenna, you would find him and stamp his beautiful, perfectly chiselled face into the dust.

"Témì? Are you there?"

"Yes, I am. What's up? I am sure she has a big butt. That's your spec."

Ikenna chuckled. "Yes, she has both back and front but I like her mostly because she reminds me of you. We really vibe."

"What's her name?"

"Ìdarà."

"Okay. Hope you are serious about her."

"Yes, oh, I am in my final year. I have to think about the future."

"Just don't break her heart. I am tired of avoiding all the girls you have hurt."

"You know I am a good guy."

"You are. You just happen to fall for many girls."

"No. A girl breaks my heart, and then another mends it."

"Lucky for some. I can't believe I am here in Ifẹ̀ by myself."

"Yeah, that sucks. I am sorry Bobby flaked on you, just as I predicted."

"Good night."

"Good night, my good Témì."

"Fuck you!"

"Is a professor's daughter allowed to swear? I'll call your father, young lady, and tell him his precious angel uses bad words."

"Byeeeeeee." You turned over in bed and closed your eyes with a smile.

The next day, when you tried to reach Ikenna, he was unavailable. He sent a text an hour later about going on a date with Ìdarà. Then he went quiet. Ikenna must have told his new babe about you, because two weeks later, he sent you another text to explain that he needed time to focus on his relationship and that Ìdarà wasn't comfortable with him having a female best friend. And so that friendship ended as well.

Your graduation was set to take place in November. No one had mentioned whether Ládùn would be there, so you asked her the next time she called.

"Ládùn, won't you come for my graduation?"

"You're graduating already? Covid didn't stop your school? That's impressive!"

"Sis, it's our school. You studied here too, don't forget."

You heard her chuckle on the other end of the line. "Témì, you know that the restrictions on travelling haven't been lifted. Besides, Lagos-Ìbàdàn Expressway is usually congested and everyone is angry, not to mention the soldiers that will be placed on the roads."

"Okay *now*, don't worry."

"Send me your account number. I'll send you a gift."

"Ahhh. Thank you, sis."

"Don't tell Mummy or Daddy."

"Of course I won't; they will collect it from me."

Your father fell sick two months after your graduation. You were all required to take a Covid test.

"Is Daddy going to be okay?" you asked your mother.

"Yes, Témì. Just self-isolate, please."

You spent the time in your room watching BBL recovery videos and testimonials. You looked up the clinic Sylvia had recommended and started researching it. They had worked on a lot of celebrities, so you were in safe hands. You couldn't afford Mexico, but Lekki was a good place too. Once your surgery was done, you would stay at Ládùn's place until you figured out your next move. You planned to tell your mother after it was all done. You checked your savings account—yes, you were ready! What could possibly go wrong?

You kept your father company on the days Màámi had to work. You reminisced about the last conversation you'd had with him. You were in the kitchen making ògì and àkàrà, debating whether to use the ginger-flavoured ògì.

"Témìladé," he called out softly.

"I'm coming, sir."

You served the meal and took it to him. He sat up carefully as you placed a tray beside him on the bed.

"Thank you. Please bring me some honey, and then draw up your mother's chair from her vanity table so you can sit to face me. I want to talk to you."

"Okay, Daddy."

After he had taken a couple of mouthfuls, he pushed the plate aside. He reached for your hand and clasped it with both of his.

"My sweetheart, let me tell you a secret. Do you know I dislike pap?"

"Ah, Daddy, sorry. Let me . . ." You stood to pick up the tray.

He pulled you back to sit. "No, I dislike the white one, but this red one you made reminds me of my mother."

"Hmmm."

"I'm going to say a few things, and I want you to listen carefully."

"Okay, sir."

"Is there anything you would like to tell me?"

You cocked your head to the side. "Anything?"

"I saw a strange message from a clinic about cosmetic surgery, and they addressed it to you. It was in my email."

Shit. The clinic sent you a form and also required a next of kin's consent. You'd forged your father's signature and sent it from his email, thinking no one would notice. "Erm . . ."

"You can talk to me. You know I am your daddy."

You looked at the floor. "Daddy, I want to fix my bumbum. It makes me feel inadequate."

"Look at me. Why do you feel inadequate?"

"I am constantly embarrassed by my lack of a backside. I don't talk about it because it seems trivial to everyone else." You told him everything and what you saw when you looked at yourself in the mirror. He was quiet, and you thought he didn't understand. But he did. When you looked up, his eyes were red.

"I am sorry, Témì. I didn't know. I guess times have changed and people have forgotten how to be kind with their words. Sometimes they joke, but they do not know that it lands in a place of hurt."

You fell into his arms, and for the first time, you broke down about everything.

"I—" You wiped the snot from your nose with your dress. "I hate my body."

"Shhhh . . ." He pulled you back into his arms. His body was unusually warm.

After you had calmed down, he looked at you. "You are such a beautiful girl, Témìladé, and I'm not saying it because you are my child. It is the truth. You and your sister took your mother's face, thankfully. Now I can't say I fully understand this, but I hear you. You are waiting, Témì. You keep waiting for life instead of seizing it and going for it. Your sister left because your mother and I hurt her, and in time, you will find out why, but when you do, please forgive, and don't stay in anger. Not everyone that hurts you cares. If this surgery will give you more enthusiasm for life— which, my love, I know it may not, because you are so beautiful and you are going to be perfect as you are in the eyes of people who love you—then do it." My father paused to catch his breath.

"Please, Témì, stop waiting for Ládùn, Bòbọọ́lá, or Ikenna to escort you through life. They will meet and walk with you at different phases, but ultimately you only have yourself. The man you marry may choose to walk the path with you forever, but even then, you must put yourself first. People's opinion of you matters when it comes to character and how you present yourself. But their appraisal of your physical attributes is not your problem. You must think of the consequences and how they will not only affect you but your loved ones too. No parent wants to bury their child. Please don't do this to your mother and me."

"I just want to be seen, Daddy. I want to matter, and for the most part, it seems like the world will only see me if I have a backside," you sniffled.

"It is in your head, Témì. I see you, and your mother sees you too. Please promise me you won't dwell on things."

"Dwell?" You shuffled uncomfortably.

"Don't dwell on your feelings. I know people have hurt you, and you feel the pain. Feel it, and then move on. If possible, forget the hurt. When my mother passed away during the Ifẹ̀/Modákéké war, I felt ashamed for not being there with her, even though we were in the same city. I felt anger at the people who were supposed to protect her, who I paid to protect her, but who ran and left her. And I felt deep sorrow because she was my mother. Nevertheless, I didn't dwell too much on it. If I did, I would have stayed in Ifẹ̀ to fight, instead of going to Lagos, where I met your mother."

He looked at you as if contemplating his next words carefully. He said, "So I will give you one million naira to add to your surgery fund, but you must promise me that you will tell your mother before you have the surgery."

"Daddy, you know she will fight me."

"You need her, so please tell her and make sure Ládùn is there too."

"Ah!"

"The three of you need each other. Please promise me."

"I promise you, sir."

"Now, bring that phone of yours that you carry everywhere. I want you to record something. It is my gift to you and your sister."

The night before your father died, you heard your mother and the doctor talking in hushed tones, and even Aunty Jummai sat still, as if she had finally realised she was an unwanted visitor in the house. At three a.m., you heard Màámi crying. Aunty Jummai's screams echoed through the walls. You knew your father was gone.

"Goodbye, Daddy," you said out loud, sitting up in bed. Your door closed gently, as it always had whenever your father came to say good night. The next morning, Màámi and Aunty Jummai told you your father had died peacefully in his sleep.

"Témì, please reach out to your sister," Màámi muttered as she held you in her arms.

After the official announcement of his death on the university website, people trooped in and out of your house, and you heard many stories in between sobs. Your father had lived a great life, and he was truly loved. As with all bad news, word of his death spread like wildfire. IK and Bòbóọlá called you many times, and they came to visit, but it meant nothing to you. You wanted everyone out of your house so it could be home again. Amidst all this, you received a text from an unknown number.

Hi Témì, this is Chuka. Ikenna gave me your number. I am so sorry about your daddy. I sadly won't be able to make the funeral because of my 4th MBBS exams. I know this is out of the blue, but will you be okay with me taking you out for dinner sometime?

Was he trying to take you out because he pitied you? He called you two days later, in the afternoon. What did he want? Hadn't he already sent his sarcastic condolences?

"Hi, Témì, this is Chuka."

"Hi, Chuka, what's up?"

"I am really sorry about your dad."

"Thank you."

"I know my text seemed out of place, but I hope we can see each other soon."

"Please, let me call you back, Chuka."

The phone felt damp against your palm. You placed it under your pillow and went out to see what chores had been assigned to you in preparation for the burial.

Then Ládùn came home.

JUMMAI'S TRUTH

Nobody knows why a marriage doesn't work, not even the people in the union. It starts with some minor issues and then culminates into something that can't be saved or rebuilt. I loved Ahmed Ayinde and gave him my heart. After we got married, we didn't have help because we were being frugal with money. I tried to make friends, but it seemed everyone in Lagos was afraid of their neighbours. For the first few months, it was just me, my protruding belly, and the television when there was power supply to watch it. Otherwise, I had to wait for my husband to return, as he alone could turn on the loud generator we'd received as a wedding gift. I stared at the ceiling until he came home, inventing imaginary friends to pass the time. Then, toward the end of my pregnancy, I started to feel really low.

"Honey, can I come to work with you? I am bored."

"And what will you do while I work? Jummai, I don't want to earn the title of the man whose wife gave birth in the bank. Don't worry; I will be back early."

Soon after, everything started to unravel.

The first time Ahmed hit me, it was after our first child was born, and I was still breastfeeding. He had come home one evening only to find out that I had not made dinner.

"Jummai, you are not the first woman to have a child," he complained.

"This is true, but my feet are swollen." I was too tired to cook.

"You are just lazy."

"And you are sometimes a useless man. What kind of man does not help his wife, who is a new mother, or at least make enough money to get her a helper?"

The blow I received nearly sent me to my maker. That was not the man I had married. I figured he'd made a mistake. A hungry man is an angry man. I didn't fight back. Instead, I went into the kitchen and prepared his favourite meal—pounded yam and égúsí—my tears mingling with the yam as I pounded.

"You are the one that made me angry. How can I be working all day and not come home to a warm meal? And then you insult me. Jummai, I am your husband. You must respect me," he said into the darkness as we lay in bed later that night.

"I am sorry." I used my hands to find his member, and it was stiff and hot as I guided him into me. I forgot about the black eye and focused on the pleasure that slowly engulfed me.

Then he hit me again, after our second child turned two, and so I showed him that it was not the thing between his legs nor his broad shoulders that made him a man. We wrestled, and I won. My face might have been swollen the next day, but every part of him, including his long stick, felt the impact of my teeth and fists.

My husband said I beat him, but I wondered what he thought would happen when he smacked me across the face. That I would have taken it lying down? You hit me; I hit you. Everything is equal.

"You are a wicked woman! Do you know of any other woman who hits her husband back?" he said to me while I was pleading with him two days after our boxing match.

"I am sorry. Please, let us eat."

He never hit me again after that day, but he stopped touching me. Perhaps he would have preferred if he was the one doing all the hitting. Even Jacob wrestled with an angel, so why my husband thought it would be different with me, I don't know. I devised many ways to win him back: I cooked his favourite meals, wore my best underwear, and even sent the children to our family friend's house to give us some privacy.

When he came home one day, I knelt in front of him and made to unbuckle his belt, but he stopped me.

"Jummai, I am not in the mood. Are you going to force me to sleep with you? Where are the kids?"

"I sent them to the Alájikìs's house. Please, my love. If you hit me now, I won't fight back."

"I am not touching you again."

I struggled to my feet warily. "If you are sleeping with other women, my head will punish you."

"Please don't ever let my children sleep out of the house again. Thank you," he said as he walked away without sparing me another glance.

From that time on, Ahmed slept on the living room sofa. After three months had passed, I knew my husband wasn't going to let it go. He punished me by withholding sex, the thing he knew I needed the most. I tried several times to pleasure myself, but that didn't work. Sex was for two living beings, not one person with a dildo or fingers.

My former roommate Fa'izah, the only friend I had made aside from Observation in school, came visiting from Abuja. Fa'izah was working on starting a newspaper that would be called *Hints*, and we stayed in touch via email. We bonded over our marital struggles. Five years into her marriage, she and her husband had had a disagreement. Fa'izah went on Hajj, and when she got back, her husband had taken a second wife to teach her a lesson.

"Jummai, this man, I gave him three boys. He married another woman without my consent."

I was stunned. "Did he say why?"

"He said I didn't laugh at a stupid joke he shared with me: 'How can you tell the mother of your children that she is like a car that easily wears out, and newer models are always more attractive?' I replied, 'I may be an old model, but young boys like women like me.'"

"Ah, Fa'izah. You know better than to make such jokes."

"I don't know better! This man married me just when I turned eighteen, and he had the audacity to call me old? Fuck him! He refuses to touch me now, and he spends all his time with this new woman."

"Just keep begging him."

She didn't heed my advice. Instead, she came to Lagos to visit. During one of those lazy afternoons before my husband or the children came home, she and I decided to experiment. Nothing serious, just a few kisses and squeezes, but Ahmed walked in on us.

After my husband witnessed us kissing and touching, Fa'izah packed her bags and left in a hurry.

"I am sorry for whatever pain this will cause you. If you ever want to see me again, send me an email. I will buy your ticket," she said as she got into her taxi, her hijab perfectly framing her face. As the taxi drove off, I knew my marriage had likely departed with her, but still, I wanted to try.

That evening, while I was on my knees once again begging my husband, he gave me an ultimatum.

"I won't divorce you, but this marriage is not working, so you must leave. In return, I won't tell anyone about that abomination I witnessed when I came home. You are still the mother of my children, but I won't let you lead them astray. Jummai, you are not fit for a man's house. Your mother did a bad job in raising you. She must be rolling in her grave right now."

I didn't argue, because the children were better off with him. They were in good schools, and his mother, who sometimes stayed with us, would cater to them like they were her own.

"What you want out of life, I can't give you," he concluded.

I packed my belongings, and went to Ifẹ to live with Hassana. On my way, a preacher approached me at the motor park.

"God has not forgotten you. Your marriage may be over, but your life is not! Give your time to God!" he said vehemently, pointing a finger in my face.

I arrived at Hassana's house later that day. "Jummai, you can stay as long as you want. Tító and I are happy to have you," my sister said. It was the first time we had seen each other since I had attended her last child's christening. I was glad she didn't throw me out. Later that night, when they thought I was asleep, I snuck up to their door and listened. I heard her complaining to the professor that she would rather they rented a house for me.

"But my love, she is your sister."

"I know, but she is not someone I am comfortable living with."
So Hassana was lying when she said she was happy to have me?

"Hassana, she is obviously going through a lot. Let's just try to be there for her."

"I don't understand why you are always so kind, even to people who don't deserve it."

I heard him move, and then Hassana moaned. I walked back into my room as I heard the bed start to squeak. At least I now had a place to rest my head. That was all I needed.

Hassana and her family went to church only once a week but, since I'd found God, that was not enough for me. I decided to find a church that could fuel my fire. After five Sundays of going from church to church, I found a white garment church on Ede Road. The music, the women shaking their buttocks, the sometimes-rhythmic clapping as the head of the church spoke in a trance, all enthralled me. The problems in my life started to melt away the moment I joined that church.

In the first year after Ládùn stormed out, I waited for that badly trained child to apologise for drawing a knife on me. I waited in vain. She didn't even send me a text. No one spoke about her, and I didn't want to be called the nosy sister, so I didn't ask Hassana. I kept myself busy in the kitchen and continued my catering job, which had helped my cash flow since I left Lagos. I listened to Professor in the evenings as he shared his views on international politics with me. The year passed without any excitement, until I met Anu.

She was one of the hottest hairdressers in Ilé-Ifẹ̀. I liked to keep my hair in braids, while Hassana wore a low cut that emphasised her oval face, and Témì was always in her demonic wigs. The hairdresser I had been using had moved to Iléshà, so I needed a new one.

"How did you get my number?" Anu's voice was firm yet kind.

"I got it from Mummy Ṣọlá. Sorry, Dr. Fáshọla."

"Oh, she's a good customer. If you want to do braids, please come tomorrow morning at six. If you are late and the students from the university get here before you, I will be busy until seven p.m."

"Okay, ma."

Anu's shop was in Mayfair. I woke up the next day at five thirty a.m., showered quickly, and got Hassana to drive me there.

"Jummai, you are going this early to have your hair done? Can't she do home service?"

"I didn't ask. Please just drop me off. E má binú."

Upon getting there, I strained my eyes to see through the fog. Her tiny shop perched on a bend in the road. It had one standing fan, two hair dryers, and a couple of magazines lying around.

"Good morning. Please wait outside; I'll call you once I am ready."

I obeyed, braving the early morning cold.

After what seemed like an eternity, she called out, "Come in, ma." I went in, and she put a small stool out for me to sit on.

"What kind of style are you looking to have?"

"All-back àdìmólè, with attachments at the end."

She put my head in her lap and started to weave.

I didn't know how to react, so I waited for the smell from her vagina to hit me before I voiced my displeasure. But nothing came. She was blissfully clean, and I had to stop myself from putting my tongue out to taste her underwear. I spent the next sixty minutes inhaling from her pussy, and I was in heaven.

She was done in an hour. I looked in the mirror and examined my hairstyle from side to side. I could see my veins sticking out, but she had plaited the hair well, so I had no complaints. I would use Robb balm to soften my edges later.

"Will you eat some moin-moin? It is the least I can offer you for making you come out this early," she offered as I gathered my things to leave.

"Yes, please," I replied, grateful for the opportunity to stay with her a little bit longer.

Anu served me from a cooler that looked like it had seen better days. When I scooped the moin-moin into my mouth, it was surprisingly delicious. The salt was moderate, and the crayfish and egg teased my tongue. I quickly devoured it.

A clean woman who could cook! I nearly came undone in my underwear. I stole glances at her as she busied herself, making pap on the stove in the corner of her shop. Anu had short, thick hair and was taller than me, with strong legs sticking out from under the Ankara skirt that danced around her knees. As she sucked on the hot pap and bit into the moin-moin, her butter-coloured teeth showed. She made small talk, but my palms were sweaty from thinking about how it would feel to touch her legs. I imagined the both of us lying on a mat together under the night sky. She took the empty plate from me, and our fingers touched briefly, sending electric waves through me. Soon her shop started to fill up. We were no longer alone.

I knew from that moment that I was going to keep coming to her shop. I found many excuses to have my hair done regularly.

"Anu, my hair is rough *o*."

"Sorry, ma. Come on Saturday."

I didn't care about the headache of having my hair constantly restyled, because I was able to breathe the same air as hers every two weeks. Anu told me she was part Hausa, part Yoruba. Her parents also lived in Ilé-Ifẹ̀. She had gotten married to the first man who came to ask for her hand, and he moved her parents into a one-bedroom in Ede. I told her about my children, and I may have implied that my husband was dead. She didn't dig deep, and I was glad to focus on the future. Anu invited me to her church, and we would go to a vigil at the end of every month, never mind that the prophet was constantly seeing visions about my husband and me getting back together.

The second year after Ládùn left, I started a forty-day fast and prayed to God to deliver me from my disease of liking both men and women.

"Aunty Jummai, are you fighting with us? Why are you cooking and not eating? Or did your sister offend you? Please eat," Professor said on the twentieth day of my fast. Hassana continued eating. As long as the food was on the table, she wasn't bothered about what I did. That man was an angel.

After forty days, I went to see Anu, hoping the spirit of God had delivered me. *Na lie!* The moment I saw her, I wanted to carry her to a corner and kiss her senseless.

"Jummai, why you no pick up my calls? You get new hairdresser?" Even the way she said my name made me love her more. It took a while to get her to feel comfortable enough to stop calling me "aunty" and "ma." There were so many things I liked about her. She was hardworking, loving, and patient with her customers, including those bratty students. Anu read with me, and she never laughed at my feminist views like my husband did. I started to teach her how to write.

"You never know, one day you could be a teacher."

"No *o*, I am a hairdresser. I love hair."

I also got free hair services. She always wanted me to look good. It was hard not to fall in love with her. I spent most of my time worshipping God, befriending Anu, and making sure that Professor ate good food. He was the only one willing to talk to me. Hassana treated me like I was a visitor, much as I expected. I heard from their muted conversation that Ládùn had gotten engaged. I started to intensify my prayers. My family needed me.

Anu got pregnant, and to the surprise of our prophet alone, her husband started cheating on and beating her.

Our prophet was undeterred. "We must not give up on your husband, Anu. Tomorrow, we will get seven coconuts and break them on the rock so that the power of strange women on him will end."

Anu immediately got to work, and I went along, but I knew it was a wasted effort. God didn't answer prayers about husbands.

Anu gave birth and moved to a bigger shop in Mayfair. Business was booming, and she hired two hairstylists to assist her. She bought a small Volkswagen and was perfecting her driving with each day's commute. Through all these changes, her husband's behaviour remained constant. "I have done everything to make this man happy. Do you know he is dating the bread seller across the road? He didn't even try to look for a woman that I don't know!" She was packing up her things in the evening after her assistants had gone for the day when I stopped by to check on her.

"Sorry, dear." I watched as she nursed her baby. I felt a pang of jealousy when he latched on to her nipple. I wished it was my mouth on her nipple instead. She fed him and strapped him to her back with a wrapper.

Anu sniffled and wiped her eyes. "How could he do this to me?" I moved over to the sofa and sat beside her. My curls were dry, and the hot rollers in my hair were starting to fall off, singeing my skin, but I took her in my arms. As she looked at me with watery eyes, I put our years of friendship to the test as I lightly brushed my lips against hers. She kissed me back, and it would have gone even further, but Jesus stopped us.

Anu left her husband just before the onset of the pandemic. I spent more and more time with her. I would go directly to her shop after I'd made all my food deliveries for the day. Even on the days when I didn't have to work, I would find excuses to go into town. I pretended to be an apprentice hairdresser so that my daily visits to her shop were justified and her nosy assistants would stop their prying. We looked after her child together, and I gradually stopped missing my children so much.

"You will spoil this child if you keep picking him up every time he cries."

"Anu, he is your son, but he is mine as well."

One afternoon in June, Anu said, "I am moving to Mayfair so I can be closer to my shop and to you."

"I don't think you should have left your husband," I told her.

"What nonsense, Jummai! The man cheated on me every day and beat me whenever I complained, so what should I have stayed for?"

"If you can, women should stay for their children."

"My child is with me, and my husband can see him when he wants to."

"So you are moving here without a husband, and then what?"

"Jummai, what is this now? Are you not the one saying the man is useless?"

"Yes, but in my opinion, most men are useless—not just your husband."

"Please come and be going. I have money, and I have my child and you."

"Anu, you can't be so naïve! What do you think is going to happen here? You think that in Ilé-Ifẹ̀ they will applaud us because we do what we please? They will burn both of us. Don't be dense. If my husband hadn't beaten me, I would have stayed and managed his uselessness."

Anu and I didn't see each other for two weeks. I buried myself in the kitchen and catering-jobs chores. I missed Anu, so I swallowed my pride and went to her. Her assistants told me she had travelled to Èkìtì.

I sent her a text.

Dear A,
I am sorry. I should not have told you the truth. Please come
back home to me.
Jummai

She didn't respond.

Weeks turned to months, then I heard from one of her neighbours that she had sold the business and moved to Ondo. I was a wreck! Food lost its taste, and life became dull. I called, texted, and even travelled to Ondo. Anu wouldn't see me. She replied to my text in December.

Jummai,
I married another man.
I am now pregnant.
Goodbye.

When did she meet the man? Was he okay with her having a child from her last marriage? I had so many questions I wanted to ask her, but I let it be and mourned our love in peace. I travelled to Lagos to visit my children, but my husband wouldn't let me see them.

"You are very stubborn. When I am convinced you are truly remorseful and submissive, you can come back. You and I both know that until you stop sinning, you can't see the children," Ahmed said.

"I can take you to court."

"Yes, you can, but are you that selfish? Your children will lose the lives they have now if you move them to Ifẹ. Let's not forget that my crime is domestic abuse. Yours is lesbianism. You will definitely spend a longer time behind bars. You may find many women like you there, though."

"At least let the children come to visit me, please. I am begging you."

"You have to plead with all my family members whom you have disrespected."

"Okay, I will." I came back to Ifẹ with my tail between my legs. At the end of January, sickness arrived in our home. I did all I could spiritually to keep Professor alive. I had never prayed for anyone the way I prayed for him. I hired prophets. I cried, and I fasted. I made promises to leave women alone. Nothing worked. By February, he was dead.

I knew God was angry with me—maybe because I wasn't there for my sister the first time. When Hassana and Professor had informed me about what happened all those years ago, I wept. I locked myself in my room and tore at my hair, asking myself what I was doing the night a man forced himself on my sister.

Was I chasing Observation?

Was I writing exams?

Was I burning another batch of letters Hassana had sent to me?

I kept hoping to remember so I could punish myself, but my memory failed me just like I failed my sister.

I knew Professor had healed her and my tears and sympathy came too late, but I made a promise to myself to help her with Témì. I would save Témì from her demons even if it was the last thing I did.

part four

TOMORROW, WE SAVE TÉMÌ

DR. ANYADIKE'S OPINION MATTERS

Dr. Anyadike was not really a morning person, but his permanently smiling face led people to believe he was available to them, especially since he was a doctor. If only they knew what was going on behind that smile. Nigerians would wake you up when they had even the smallest medical "crisis" on their hands. He no longer fell for their theatrics, which was why he blamed himself for answering Hassana's call at four a.m.

"Good morning, Doctor. I hope I didn't wake you up?" Hassana asked softly. Never mind that he had only gone to bed an hour before. The response he wanted to give was "Of course you didn't. I was awake, preparing a concoction for my patients. Please don't be daft." Instead, he said, "Good morning, Hassana. What's going on?"

He listened but was more focused on the whistling sound from his wife's nostrils, as she snored gently. He felt his anger shift slightly toward his wife. He made a mental note to ask her to come to the clinic later, so that he could look into it. A snoring wife meant no sleep for him.

Part of the reason the phone call from Hassana irritated the doctor was because he had dealt with a similar phone call the day before. "Doctor, I am worried. The multivitamins are not working, my daughter is not eating, and I can't sleep." The disturbance was from one of his most difficult patients. Did she think waking him up at the hour witches converge would solve her problem? That was a patient who refused to subscribe to his hospital's premium plan, who preferred to go into town to buy the drugs prescribed at a much cheaper price, yet she kept sending him pictures and videos of her daughter.

After reminding himself why he loved medicine, Dr. Anyadike responded calmly, "You can bring her in later today, madam."

"Okay. We will be there by seven a.m."

"The clinic opens at nine a.m., madam."

"This is an emergency, Doctor."

He ended the call and blocked her number. He then asked his assistant to send out a bulk SMS to all his patients, reminding them that they may only reach out to them within working hours. Clearly, his assistant left the Tóyèbís out since she knew Tító was his best friend.

Why else would Hassana wake him up at four a.m.? He forced himself to listen to her. Wait, did she just say Témì was going to reconstruct her yansh? There was a spirit troubling the new generation. They were forever smoking, drinking, and emphasising their need for vibes. The other day, he had caught his son smoking at the back of their house. "Dad, you and I are not vibing, so I need some blunt to chill," Udoka explained.

"Oh! So weed will help you understand me better?" Dr. Anyadike queried him.

"Yup."

"Udoka, you are possessed."

Perhaps the doctor was too hard on the boy, but he was his only child. If Udoka didn't turn out well, Dr. Anyadike's family would laugh at him and the Yoruba woman that he married despite their pleas that he marry an Igbo woman. Hassana's phone call confirmed that it wasn't only his son who needed help. Somehow that gave him relief.

Hassana called out, "Doctor, are you there?"

"Yes, I am."

"Please, I need your help. Témì is your child as well."

"I'll come in a few hours. We will talk to her. Please stop crying," he said.

"Thank you, sir."

They said their goodbyes, and Dr. Anyadike rested on the headboard. He knew he would not sleep anymore. Grief swallowed him. He reminisced on the conversation he had had with Tító after his friend was diagnosed with hypertension. Dr. Anyadike told Tító to start doing regular checkups.

"I am a strong man, Anyadike," Tító countered when the advice was offered.

"Tító, you are over sixty. You need to be doing diagnostics twice a year."

"I feel fine. I don't have time to go to the clinic."

"But you have time to go to the staff club and ASUU conventions. My friend, your priorities are not straight."

Dr. Anyadike had also warned him not to go to the political conference where he caught Covid.

"The fight for our people is continuous," Tító had insisted.

"Tító, this country is gone. Fight for yourself," Dr. Anyadike responded.

"I was not made to think for myself alone."

"That's why you have remained a middle-earning professor although you studied at the best universities. You are too invested in people. I care only for my family, and even then, I make sure my wife and son understand that I am not responsible for their happiness and survival."

"You love Bùsólá, and I know you are crazy about Udoka."

"I think I might hate him because he is so spoilt. I do love Bùsólá, though. We are the only men who dared to marry the women we love."

"How lucky we are!"

Tító's first and possibly only love was his family, which was perhaps why Ládùn's absence was extremely hard on him. One evening at the club, Tító confided in his friend. "Anyadike, my daughter has refused to come home. My wife is angry, and Témì is just looking to fill her absence with those fair-weather friends of hers." It was just him and Dr. Anyadike, without the drunken crowd.

"I am sorry, man."

"It is fine. I am grateful that I have a family. I just wish we were all under the same roof." Dr. Anyadike could see the pain in his eyes.

Bùsólá's snore brought Dr. Anyadike back to the present. He glanced at his wife and sighed. The nightgown had slipped off both her arms, and her breasts were fully exposed. He pressed his erection down, then headed for his home office. He had work to do. Part of what made Dr. Anyadike decide to act swiftly was the twinge of guilt he felt for not raising Témì's body issues with her parents after she was admitted many years ago to his hospital. He had thought it strange that she was worried about her weight and assumed she would grow out of whatever childish thoughts fogged her mind. Apparently that had not happened.

PROPHET, PLEASE PRAY IT AWAY!

Prophet Túndé communicated with Sister Jummai in dreams.
She had appeared to him the night before, asking to see him, so he
was not shocked when she showed up at the church that day. He
was waiting for her. "Hallelujah, Sister Jummai."

"Prophet, please, our house is on fire. The devil wants to ruin
Témì's life."

"That devil will die in Jesus's name."

"Amen!"

"Now, tell me what the issue is with our child."

The prophet always thought Sister Jummai could have easily
been an actress. She didn't speak with words alone. Her arms,
legs, and even her backside conveyed the message. The prophet
didn't watch television, but he watched Sister Jummai—she was
his holy entertainment. Whenever a matter bothered Sister Jummai, she started by making a deep sound in her throat, her chest
heaving, then threw her hands behind her head, clasped them together, and parted her legs as if the news was a baby that she was
going to deliver. Then she sat back down and started speaking.

That day was no different as she shared her dilemma with him.

"Témì wants to allow the world into her body. She wants to open her body with a knife and put fat in her bumbum. Prophet, a child we have invested our lives in wants to destroy my family. She wants to do this so that a man can love her."

Prophet Túndé didn't fully understand what she meant, but if it had made Sister Jummai that upset, perhaps it was time to start praying against it.

"I will begin a seven-day fast for Témì," he told her as she finally sat down.

She jumped up again. "Prophet, please come and talk to her, pray with her, and take the demon away!"

As the prophet continued to watch Sister Jummai's theatrics, he came to the conclusion that the devil seemed to create new problems for every generation. *Why else would anyone choose to re-create herself after our maker had made her?* The prophet already felt many young girls were strange beings with the wings they wore on their eyes. Most of his church members were practically naked with their see-through sutanas, but he couldn't do anything to stop them, because if he lost them, his church would lose its selling point. After all, young men came to his church to see which naked sister they could become one with at the altar of Christ. The devil truly never slept. Prophet Túndé's wife looked like a man, but he loved her. His daughter looked like his wife, but he was sure someone would love her too. So why did Témì think she would not find love with a flat backside?

BIG SISTER LÁDÙN

Knock, knock.

I peeped through the keyhole. "Who is at my door this early?"

"Please open the door. It is me." My mother stood in the shadows. How did she know where to find me? Perhaps Témì told her. *Why, Témì? Why?*

As my mother stepped into the room, her bloodshot eyes matched mine. My mother followed the warm glow from the nightstand lamp to find the chair next to the desk and sat down. She looked leaner. If the situation hadn't been so dire, I would have smiled at how Témì had managed to humble our mother. "Good morning, ma."

"Good morning, Ládùn. I am here to talk about Témì. It seems you have been avoiding me."

"Mummy, you've seen me every day since I got here."

"Hmm . . ."

I walked back to sit on the bed.

"We have a lot to talk about, but first, what are we going to do about your sister?"

"I don't know." Even as I spoke, I heard how tired I sounded.

"We need to be united on this matter. That is why I am here."

"If she is determined, I don't think we can stop her," I replied.

"Témì looks up to you. Where else did she get this idea of going to Lagos?"

"I am not to blame for Témì's—"

"It is not important who is to blame," my mother cut in. "We all have our fair share. So let us stand together on this matter so she knows she is going nowhere. In fact, I don't think you should allow her to stay with you in Lagos."

"Mummy, I don't understand you. Do you think that will stop her?"

"Ládùn, when you become a mother, you can raise your children as you see fit."

"I will do my best not to lie to them!"

"I didn't lie. What did you want from me? Why are you always trying to pick a fight?" My mother began pacing up and down the room. "Your father came into my life, and what was supposed to be pain became joy. You became our world! Then you left us!"

"I didn't leave by choice!" I swallowed around the tightness in my throat. I squeezed the bedsheets.

My mother stopped in her tracks and pointed at me. "You abandoned your family!"

"I didn't want to! I was heartbroken!"

"Over that coward? A boy that didn't even fight for you?" Her voice grew quiet. "Ládùn, that marriage would have been a sham."

The quietness discomfited me. "Why did you not tell me sooner? Why was Mofé's situation the reason you had to confess everything?" I was tired of fighting with my mother.

Her voice broke. "We were going to tell you. We never intended for you to find out that way."

"Please don't cry, Mum."

She moved to the bed and sat beside me. "Ládùn, I am sorry I didn't tell you about your father before the Mofé situation, and I am truly sorry that I let you leave the house that night. Please forgive me. It has been five years. Please. I don't know how to help your sister. I need your help. I . . . I know we have a lot to work out. Please, Ládùn. I can't lose both my children and my husband."

I caught her as she sank toward the carpeted floor. She was so light. *When did she last eat?* "No, Màámi."

My mother's eyes opened wide. I had never called her that before. "Màámi, please get up. I forgive you." Màámi's eyes brimmed with fresh tears. I continued. "Don't worry about me. I am on board with whatever decision we make concerning Témì. I also don't want her to go through with the surgery."

"Then it is settled. Thank you, my daughter."

"I am really sorry about Daddy. I know you loved each other very much, and I can't begin to imagine the pain you are feeling."

"He loved you too, Ládùn. That man loved us all. Please come home sometimes. Come and stay at the house." She opened her arms. "I have not hugged you since you came home."

I leaned into her embrace. After a few minutes, Màámi pulled away and softly touched my face. "Let me go now. I called Dr. Anyadike. He says he will be at our place by eight a.m. You can come and join us when you are ready."

"Okay, Màámi."

She walked to the door and then turned to look at me. "I love you, Ládùn. I love you and your sister. Sometimes my actions may fail to—"

I didn't let her finish. "I love you too, Màámi."

She smiled at me and slipped out.

As soon as my mother left, I fell into a peaceful sleep for the first time since my father's death.

TÉMÌ

You finally got your moment with your sister very early the next morning. Your head was still ringing with the aftereffects of the cookies Ṣọlá had given you, and Ládùn's voice sounded hollow.

"I hope I didn't wake you. I know it's barely six," Ládùn said, walking toward you.

You sat up, wiping the sleep from your eyes. "It's fine. First Màámi, now you. Who knew bumbum was all I needed to get you people's attention?"

"You are my sister, Témì. You will always have my attention."

You stuck out your lower lip. "Was it something I did that made you leave? No one will tell me anything."

"No, Témì, don't be silly. That would have been wicked, placing such a burden on your young shoulders." Ládùn stared at you from the foot of the bed. She sighed, knowing she had not said what you really wanted to hear. Her voice was quieter now. "Témì, my leaving that night had nothing to do with you." She laid her hand on top of yours, squeezing it. "You are my sister. I have missed you so much, and I am here now. I won't leave again."

You pulled your hand from under Ládùn's. As usual, she'd

danced her way around your question. "What do you mean by you won't leave again?"

"I mean I am here for you."

"Ládùn, if you want to be there for me, let me stay in your house when I fix my bumbum." You looked at her, expecting a rebuttal. You didn't care because having your bumbum fixed was the only thing that mattered to you.

"Témì, Lagos is not what you think it is," Ládùn said quietly.

"*Shebi* you left? Let me leave too, and then if Lagos doesn't work, I will make a heroic return after five years and say I want to stay."

"Fine," Ládùn mumbled. *Good, feel the pain too.*

Your sister interrupted your thoughts. "Témì, I need to ask you this." You lifted your chin slightly, indicating that she should go ahead. "Are you fixing your butt to impress boys?"

"Maybe? Most importantly, sis, this is what I want." You were as honest as you could possibly be.

"Okay, I can respect that." Ládùn pulled you into a warm embrace. You let yourself melt into her hug. You didn't know what that moment fully meant, but you felt a weight lift from your shoulders. You saw a future in which you could make your own choices. You saw your family clapping approvingly. It meant everything to you. In her arms, you found succour. Ládùn left after you started to doze off.

You woke again much later that morning to liquid dripping on your face. When you were able to see, the blurry image turned out to be Aunty Jummai's spiritual leader. "Get out, you demon of bumbum! You demon of cosmetic surgery!" Prophet Túndé screamed, sprinkling olive oil all over you. "This child does not belong to you, you dirty, fake spirit. Get out and catch fire!"

If you weren't wiping your face and trying to look for your phone, you would have laughed. Where was it? You scrambled around in your bed and slid your hand between the wall and your bed frame. Where was your phone?

Suddenly, he grabbed you, dragged you out of bed, and forced you to your knees. You caught a whiff of his perfume mixed with the smell of whatever he had been eating as he ordered out demons and devils.

"Amen!" Aunty Jummai was standing in the doorway with a Bible pointed directly at you. Your mother was behind her, as if unsure of what was happening. She had your phone in one hand and was holding your handbag in the other. Eventually, the prophet stopped spitting on you.

"Màámi, can I please have my phone—"

"Sister Témì, please focus!" Prophet Túndé cut in.

"We have seized your phone and your bag. You are not going anywhere!" Aunty Jummai said as she closed the door.

"Am I going to be held against my will?" you screamed.

"No, you are here so that we can understand." Màámi's muffled response came through the door.

"How do you want to understand when you are all reacting like this?" you asked her.

"Sister Hassana, don't worry, I will chase out these demons!" He hefted a large Bible and shook it in your face. "Let us look into the Bible. No woman worried about her buttocks there. Did Deborah win the war with her buttocks? Did Jacob notice Rachel's yansh? Did Esther win the heart of the king with hers?"

"No!" Aunty Jummai responded with gusto.

Those women didn't need to win anything with their buttocks because of the society they were in. Times are different!

A fresh sprinkle of olive oil reminded you of your predicament. Was he trying to add acne to your list of challenges? Your skin was one of your best features. The man had to go.

"Sister Témì, the devil is leading you astray."

"No, Prophet, sir. Respectfully, it is your congregation you should worry about. One of your members was on a blog last week for beating his wife in Sábó. I am sure my sin is smaller than his. Please worry about your church, sir!"

Prophet Túndé's eyes darkened as if you had somehow morphed into the devil, and he was ready to take you on. His lips shook as he pointed at you, roaring, "You are going to hellfire with your fake body!"

The muffled voices in the hallway rose as your door closed behind Prophet Túndé's retreating form. You had just angered Aunty Jummai's prophet. That made you smile.

You stopped by the bathroom to wash your face and caught sight of yourself in the mirror. You looked like you felt: tired, angry, and still a little high. You didn't have time to take it all in because you heard your name, as if they were coming for you. You rushed into the living room in time to see Prophet Túndé gathering his things. Dr. Anyadike was seated with your mother, his face lined with a frown. You also saw Barrister Chima, Aunty Jummai, Big Mummy, and a picture of your late father seated on his chair.

"Good morning, everyone."

"Who is everyone?" Aunty Jummai said, talking fast in her

fury. "See what I am saying? This girl is spoilt rotten. Sit down, my friend. Your fake greeting means nothing. You were very rude to Prophet Túndé." The woman was more Yoruba than anyone else.

Big Mummy hissed. "Can't you greet us one by one? Honestly, I blame your mother for this bad behaviour."

"Let me be on my way. Don't worry. I will pray the cosmetic surgery demon away, Sister Jummai," Prophet Túndé said, hurrying out of the house.

The doctor spoke next. "Témì, please sit down." The sweet aroma of the spicy jollof left over from yesterday danced near your nose as you sat on the low stool they had put out for you in the middle of the room, as if they were going to start an initiation ceremony. "Your mother woke me up early today with news that unsettled me. I told her it couldn't be true because I know you to be very responsible, respectful, and considerate. You are the one child that has managed not to break her parents' hearts. I am here to assuage your mother's fears because I know it is quite impossible that you would make such a ridiculous decision as to go under the knife. I am quite disappointed in you, Témì."

It was ironic hearing him say this, given the circumstances with his son, Udoka. You struggled to keep yourself from laughing.

"Are you laughing? Doctor, please forget it. She has broken our hearts; just help us advise her," Aunty Jummai said. At that point, you wanted to ask if they had considered getting you a therapist instead of the paediatrician who had watched you grow up.

Dr. Anyadike continued, "I know you have had fears about your body, but you are only twenty—"

"Bumbum will eventually give you bad knees! Do you think I am happy with the load on my back?" Big Mummy interjected.

Ládùn floated in just then, dressed in ádìre with a matching headband holding her long braids in place.

"Good morning, Màámi, Aunty Jummai, Big Mummy, Barrister, Doctor, sir." She bent her knees a little, a show of respect.

"My ever-beautiful Ládùn, please sit," the doctor replied.

Aunty Jummai interrupted the meeting to serve hot jollof and Titus fish with fried plantain. "Please, let us eat while we discuss this child's matter," she said.

"I am not hungry," your mother said quietly.

"We will still serve our guests, won't we?" Aunty Jummai retorted.

Your mother lifted her head. "Jummai, please hold your tongue today. If you annoy me, I will forget that my husband has just died and throw you out!" Her tone was sharp enough to make everyone eat silently.

You go, Màámi. Put her in her place! If she wasn't fighting you, you would have given Màámi a thumbs-up. Instead, you continued to look down as you spoke. "Aunty Jummai, please, can I have some?"

She looked surprised that you dared to ask. "Yes, go and get the plate I covered in the kitchen."

You saw Ládùn struggling to hide her smile. She was probably smiling at your audacity. You were hungry, and your head was still feeling very light. You walked into the kitchen, standing by the counter to eat.

"Hey, I tried calling you a while ago." Ládùn interrupted your thoughts.

"Màámi took my phone."

"Are you okay?"

"I am. I am just hungry."

"Okay. Sorry about all this."

"Oh! It's fine."

Ládùn put down her plate and stood for a minute as if she had more to say, then she appeared to change her mind and left the room. Her perfume lingered and wrapped you in its warmth as you bit into the fried plantain.

"Témì, come back here!"

"Yes, ma." You resumed your sitting position with your head bowed.

"In all my forty-three years on earth," Big Mummy started. Aunty Jummai cleared her throat, but Big Mummy ignored her. It was the fifth year that Big Mummy was turning forty-three. "I have never heard of what you said yesterday. What kind of child says to her only living parent that she is going to open her bumbum? Now we are asking you to be reasonable. We have even brought a doctor to you to explain that this madness will kill you, and you are still insisting. Do you know that my Alfa sent me a message this morning? I praise Allah for his wisdom. He saw a bad omen in his dream."

"Jésù Kristì," Aunty Jummai screamed.

"I have asked Alfa to start a seven-day prayer for you. Even though my ègbón left me nothing, I will not desert his children." Big Mummy clutched her purse tight, making the green veins on her hands more obvious. The wrinkles on each finger looked dry, and her ring was starting to fade. "I came from town this early because your mother is a good person. She is the only Hausa woman in this house who has respect for me. I came for her and my late brother. Why has this madness overcome you? If you are mourning your father, then mourn like a normal person."

"Màámi, please, can I have my phone?" You half expected her to refuse, but instead, she leaned forward and handed it over. Your fingers touched, and she finally looked at you. Her bloodshot eyes had tears swimming in them. Your own eyes were filled with questions.

Dr. Anyadike cleared his throat. "I have brought some materials for you to read while I share some vital information on the dangers of this journey you are determined to embark on. First of all, many women who have gone under the knife have died. Do you want your mother to lose you as well? Please pity her. Secondly, why would you put your money into something like that? Most women who have done this swear they will never do it again. Témì, I am a doctor, and I know how hard it is to undergo a surgery, let alone one that is purely cosmetic."

"Thank you, Doctor."

"So now that you know the implications of what you are going to do, are you still going to do it?" Aunty Jummai asked.

"Yes, Aunty Jummai, yes, Doctor, yes, Màámi, yes, Ládùn, yes, Big Mummy," you responded.

"You are a very silly girl. Now you are mocking your elders?" Aunty Jummai quipped, wagging her fingers at you.

"Aunty, let's hear from Témì, please," Ládùn said in a loud whisper.

"What can she possibly have to say?" Aunty Jummai shouted.

Big Mummy glared at you. "Alhamdulillah! At least for once, your mother and I agree that you are a spoilt child. Both of you—but it looks like Ládùn is even better behaved. She just likes to leave her family in the dust."

Màámi finally spoke. "We have brought your late father into this meeting since you will not let him rest! I want you to keep staring at that picture so that as you try to destroy us, you can see your father's face."

You grimaced. The only person who understood you was now six feet under, and the family was going crazy over a decision that was not going to change.

"Did you not hear your mother?" Big Mummy's voice boomed.

You looked around before speaking carefully. "What is the point of just existing? I want to *live*. This is why I am fixing my buttocks," you said to them.

"You won't be alive to live, dear! Did you not hear the doctor? Do you want us to bury you?" Big Mummy responded. She continued, "Come, Témì, since your father died, I have not seen you cry. Now you want to open your buttocks—" She paused as if the words were too heavy, and chose instead to swallow them, then turned to face your mother. "Hassana, are you sure this child is not possessed?"

Ládùn answered before Màámi could speak. "People must grieve as they like, Big Mummy. We can't all be screaming around the house because we are sad. Témì is sad. She has barely eaten since I came home. She is also now saying she wants something. Let us treat the matters separately." Aunty Jummai sighed loudly. You could see she was struggling to keep her composure. Ládùn ignored her.

"It is only in this house that children answer back to their elders! You people have spoilt your youngest. Now you are on your own." Big Mummy pointed a finger at Màámi.

You'd had enough, so you stood to face them all. "How can you ask me how I came to be this way? Everywhere I look, the perfect image for a woman is projected—on TV, social media, and elsewhere! Màámi, you like that comedian who always puts curvy women in his videos, don't you? Aunty Jummai, you laugh at his jokes. I want to look like those women. I also want to be idolised! I deserve to be, and I am going to ensure I get that, as well as the other good things that will happen to me the moment I become perfect. Big Mummy, I know my daddy is dead. I was there, and I am still here. I can't bring him back, but I can make myself happier."

"What is this life coming to, Lord?" Aunty Jummai knelt, raising her hands in surrender. Big Mummy scrunched her face as if she had tasted something nasty.

You looked around the room. "I have some questions. I am sure I won't get the answers. I know how we roll in this family. Case in point, Ládùn."

Big Mummy hissed. "No manners at all."

"We just sweep issues under the rug, but I will ask anyway," you declared.

Ládùn's eyes pleaded with you. "But, Témì, I said sorry—"

You laughed a little. "So 'sorry' should fix five years?" She made to speak, but your raised finger stopped her. "Ládùn, this is not about you. I am just citing an example."

Ládùn visibly shrank, like you had just caned her.

"If everyone can answer the questions I ask, then I won't do the surgery." The hush in the room let you know that you had the upper hand. You faced your mother first. "Màámi, why did Ládùn leave and not come home for five years?"

You shifted your focus to Aunty Jummai next. "Aunty Jummai, why has your husband not come to get you? Who were you always going to see in town?"

You moved your gaze to Big Mummy, who was suddenly perched on the edge of her seat. "Big Mummy, where is your first husband, and why do you bleach your skin?"

Silence.

"Témì! How dare you question us!" Aunty Jummai shook with fury. She sprang up, nearly knocking her chair over and spilling the water on the stool beside her.

"Auzubillah Minashaitan Nirajeem! Hassana! You people spoilt these children!" Big Mummy clasped her hands across her chest, as if your words were arrows that had pierced her. Ládùn raised her hand to speak, as if asking for permission, but your mother stopped her.

"Erm . . . Témì, we have heard you. Go and do your surgery. We will all support you in every way we can." Màámi spoke quietly. She looked at the others in the room, who were struggling to make sense of what she had just said. "Thank you all for coming. You may leave."

"Thank you, ma," you said.

"Go to your room," she responded.

As you walked down the corridor, you caught a reflection of yourself, and your ears were no longer ringing.

If you had the guts, what would you have done to Evidence,

Truth, Chetachi, the campus bloggers, and the internet trolls, Témì? Nothing.

Those people were not wrong. You were without bumbum, and they were right to state their expectations. Once that expectation was met, perhaps people would finally see you. A small voice asked, *What will society expect you to fix next? Your left breast, which is slightly bigger than the right? Or your loud voice?* Or would you fix the accidental *h* that occasionally slipped out when you were not measuring your words? That was part of being Yoruba. You were certain there was also a scientific explanation for the loudness of Yoruba people.

As you walked back to your room, you heard raised voices. An argument was brewing again. You lay down, then realised you had left your phone on the stool. It was not worth going back and being in the eye of the storm. You were left with your thoughts. Would the bumbum make everyone finally love you?

AUTHOR'S NOTE

My dear friends,

The truth is, for a long time, my only companions were the books I read, including the Bible. Now, as a writer, I have you, my community of readers, as friends, because whether we meet or not, you have been there for me. I only hope my books are there for you on the days when you feel alone, broken, and just not ready to face the world. Thank you for all your messages, videos, emails, texts, and notes.

I wrote this book for many personal reasons, but the most important reason is the obvious pressure on the young people of today whose **Tomorrow** I fear is filled with too many expectations: for young women to be perfect, sexy, and have clear skin, and for young men to be rich, spend recklessly, and have beards! It has gotten to a point where, every time I step out, there is a familiar face with a new body or slightly altered facial features. Everyone is starting to look alike. When did perfection become the goal?

My dear young women, please understand, I am not against plastic surgery, but your bodies need time to develop. Give them time. After that, if you still don't love the growth, do what will make you happy. Fix them, exercise them, whatever, but please do it for yourself.

To all the girls who have gone under the knife to seek approval from others, I am sorry. You are enough. To the girls who went under the knife for themselves, you are bad bitches, and I salute you. I am sending you all my love through my words every time you pick up any of my books.

Love and Light,
Damilare

ACKNOWLEDGEMENTS

I am grateful to God, who walks with me on all days, especially through *the valley of the shadow of life*. I am who I am because of You, Lord. I hope I am telling the stories the way You have told them to me. I am in love with You, and I bow at Your feet always, Daddy.

I thank the women who allowed me into their lives in my imagination to tell their stories. They were open, and life took an interesting turn for me. I am so, so grateful that there are people who love my voice as a writer; for as long as you keep reading, I will keep writing.

I wrote this book while thinking of my sisters. Sisterhood is such a precious gift. I thank Oluwadunni for maturity, love, and listening ears on all days. I thank Eniolaoluwa for teaching me unconditional love and gratitude. I love you both so much.

I also wanted to pay homage to some of the places that moulded me into the person I am today—Ilé-Ifẹ̀ and Lagos. The town and city hold special places in my heart. I can't think of Ilé-Ifẹ̀ without the memories of Grandma, Aunty Funmi, Uncle Eda, Captain, and cans of Titus sardine floating freely in my memory bank. What a time it was!

I lost my grandma, Julianna Elumoye, and my aunt, Kehinde

Elumoye, while writing this book. These women helped raise me, and I share memories with them that I will forever keep close. I miss them deeply, and I hope they are resting with the Lord.

To Professor Olorode, I love you so much. I wrote Titó while thinking of you. You are such a marvel. My dear captain, I remember the tree-climbing years with you. You are loved deeply by me.

I thank Dr. Udengwu and the late Professor Foluke Ogunleye, women whose voices remind me that I must live up to my abilities. I hope I am making you both proud.

I want to thank Chimamanda Ngozi Adichie for lighting a fire in me with *Half of a Yellow Sun*, and Chimeka Garricks, one of the best writers and men I know, for EVERYTHING. Chimeka, you made this possible and I thank you.

Many thanks to Charlotte Seymour, my brilliant agent, who worked with me to beat the manuscript into shape. I thank my editors, Mina Asaam and Gretchen Schmid, and all their brilliant colleagues for their hard work in bringing my stories to readers around the world! A special thank-you to my copyeditor, Kaitlyn San Miguel, for her meticulous efforts. My deepest gratitude to my team at Pan Macmillan South Africa for their very encouraging reviews of my writing; they boosted my confidence. And to my international team, thank you for everything.

I am thankful for my love. What a profound joy it is to be loved by you! Let's keep having fun!

Finally, to my mother, Oluremi: Each time I write, I write for you. These words are yours as well. I am finally telling stories; I hope you enjoy them as much as I enjoyed yours growing up. What great joy it is that we are mother-daughter friends. Thank you for holding my hand while I wrote this book, especially on the weakest days. I love you, Màámi.

A NOTE ON THE COVER

The bar was set high with the cover design of Damilare Kuku's *Nearly All the Men in Lagos are Mad,* so the challenge to create a complementary but distinct package for her follow-up title was a tall task. With such a strong visual brand for Kuku already taking shape, the goal was to create another bold, colorful, and simple design. I wanted to continue exploring graphic lettering, and with the editor's suggestion to include some kind of unconventional representation of a woman on the cover, the perfect artist came to mind.

Artist Tschabalala Self "builds a singular style from the syncretic use of painting, printmaking, and sculpture to explore ideas surrounding the black body." Self's piece *Evening* (2019), paired with custom collaged lettering to match her style of stitching, created a cohesive design, one that continues to develop the author's visual identity and signature voice.

—Stephen Brayda

Here ends Damilare Kuku's
Only Big Bumbum Matters Tomorrow.

The first edition of this book was printed
and bound at Lakeside Book Company
in Harrisonburg, Virginia, July 2024.

A NOTE ON THE TYPE

The text in this book is set in Minion 3, part of a contemporary serif type family created by Robert Slimbach, an award-winning designer who now directs Adobe's type design program. Minion's first iteration was released in 1990 and was inspired by late Renaissance era type. Its name comes from one of the traditional names for type sizes: "minion" size was equal to seven points, or roughly two-and-a-half millimeters. Minion is highly legible, clean, and balanced, making it a popular, if conservative, choice for books. It is also used in the logos of Brown University, the Smithsonian Museum, and the Daughters of the American Revolution, as well as for the body text of Robert Bringhurst's *The Elements of Typographic Style.* Minion 3, an update released in 2018, includes Latin glyphs for several African languages, Vietnamese, and the full International Phonetic Alphabet.

HARPERVIA

An imprint dedicated to publishing international voices,
offering readers a chance to encounter other lives and other
points of view via the language of the imagination.